CLAIRE and the DRAGONS

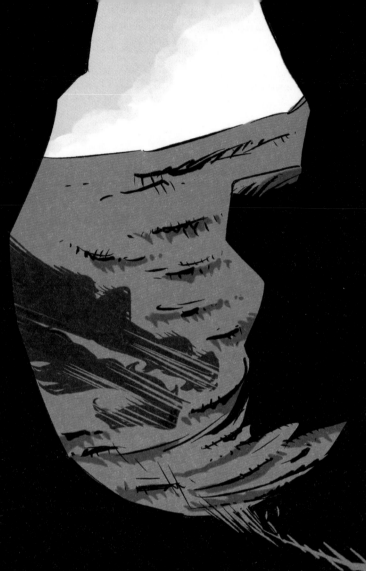

SCOUT COMICS

FB/TW/IG:
@scoutcomics

LEARN MORE AT:
www.scoutcomics.com

Brendan Deneen, *CEO*
James Haick III, *President*
Don Handfield, *CCO*
Lesa Miller, *COO*
Richard Rivera, *Exec. VP*
David Byrne, *Co-Publisher*
Charlie Stickney, *Co-Publisher*
Andrea Lorenzo Molinari, *Editorial Director*
Marcus Guillory, *Head of Design*
Trent Miller, *General Counsel*
Nicole D'Andria, *Director of Digital Content*

CLAIRE and the DRAGONS

VOLUME 1

CREATOR, WRITER, ARTIST
WANDER ANTUNES

TRANSLATION
MARJORY ABULEAC AND THATY MARIANA

SCOUT EDITOR
ANDREA LORENZO MOLINARI

SCOUT PRODUCTION
SEAN CALLAHAN

CHAPTER 1

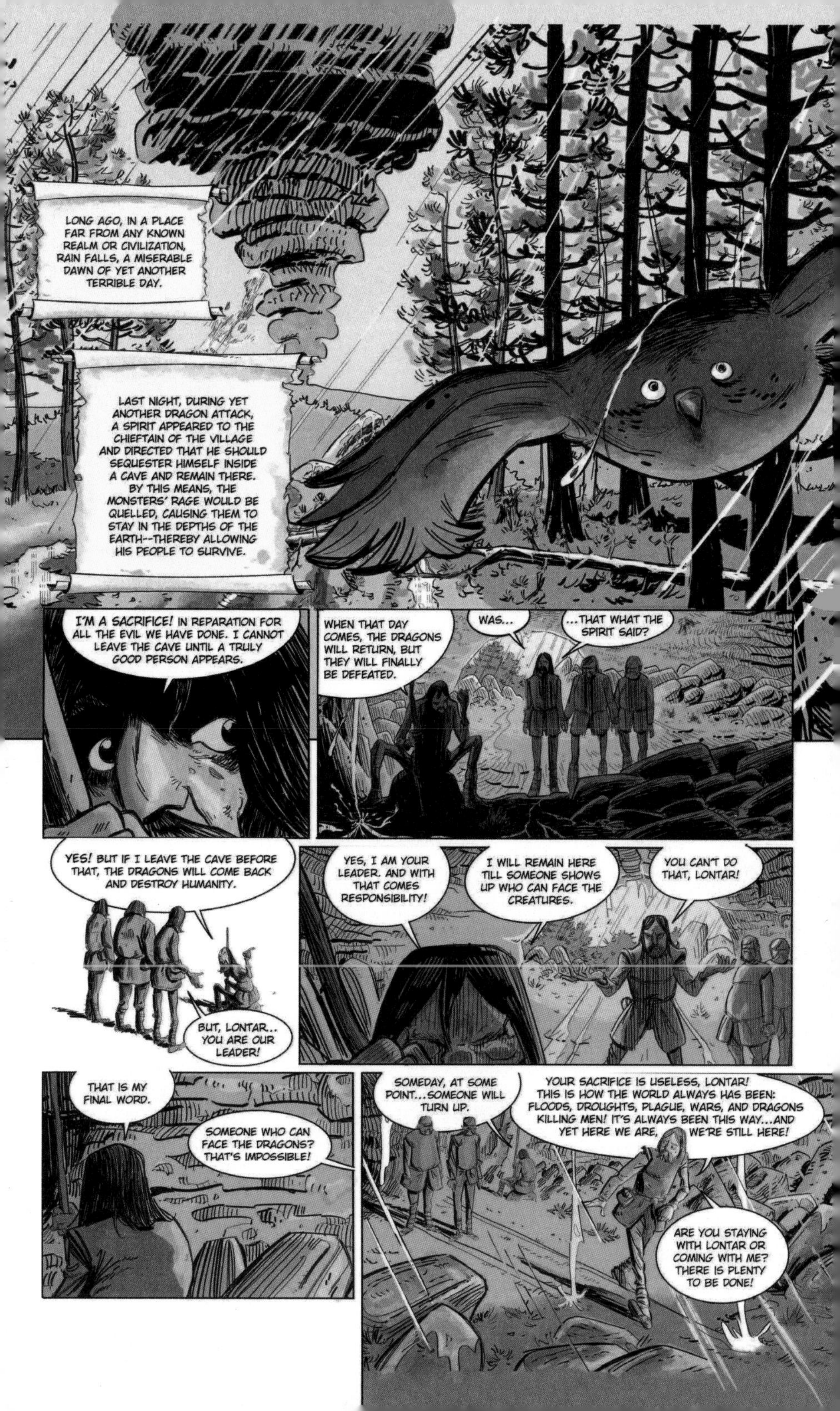

LONG AGO, IN A PLACE FAR FROM ANY KNOWN REALM OR CIVILIZATION, RAIN FALLS, A MISERABLE DAWN OF YET ANOTHER TERRIBLE DAY.
LAST NIGHT, DURING YET ANOTHER DRAGON ATTACK, A SPIRIT APPEARED TO THE CHIEFTAIN OF THE VILLAGE AND DIRECTED THAT HE SHOULD SEQUESTER HIMSELF INSIDE A CAVE AND REMAIN THERE. BY THIS MEANS, THE MONSTERS' RAGE WOULD BE QUELLED, CAUSING THEM TO STAY IN THE DEPTHS OF THE EARTH--THEREBY ALLOWING HIS PEOPLE TO SURVIVE.
I'M A SACRIFICE! IN REPARATION FOR ALL THE EVIL WE HAVE DONE. I CANNOT LEAVE THE CAVE UNTIL A TRULY GOOD PERSON APPEARS.
WHEN THAT DAY COMES, THE DRAGONS WILL RETURN, BUT THEY WILL FINALLY BE DEFEATED.
WAS...
...THAT WHAT THE SPIRIT SAID?
YES! BUT IF I LEAVE THE CAVE BEFORE THAT, THE DRAGONS WILL COME BACK AND DESTROY HUMANITY.
BUT, LONTAR... YOU ARE OUR LEADER!
YES, I AM YOUR LEADER. AND WITH THAT COMES RESPONSIBILITY!
I WILL REMAIN HERE TILL SOMEONE SHOWS UP WHO CAN FACE THE CREATURES.
YOU CAN'T DO THAT, LONTAR!
THAT IS MY FINAL WORD.
SOMEONE WHO CAN FACE THE DRAGONS? THAT'S IMPOSSIBLE!
SOMEDAY, AT SOME POINT...SOMEONE WILL TURN UP.
YOUR SACRIFICE IS USELESS, LONTAR! THIS IS HOW THE WORLD ALWAYS HAS BEEN: FLOODS, DROUGHTS, PLAGUE, WARS, AND DRAGONS KILLING MEN! IT'S ALWAYS BEEN THIS WAY...AND YET HERE WE ARE, WE'RE STILL HERE!
ARE YOU STAYING WITH LONTAR OR COMING WITH ME? THERE IS PLENTY TO BE DONE!

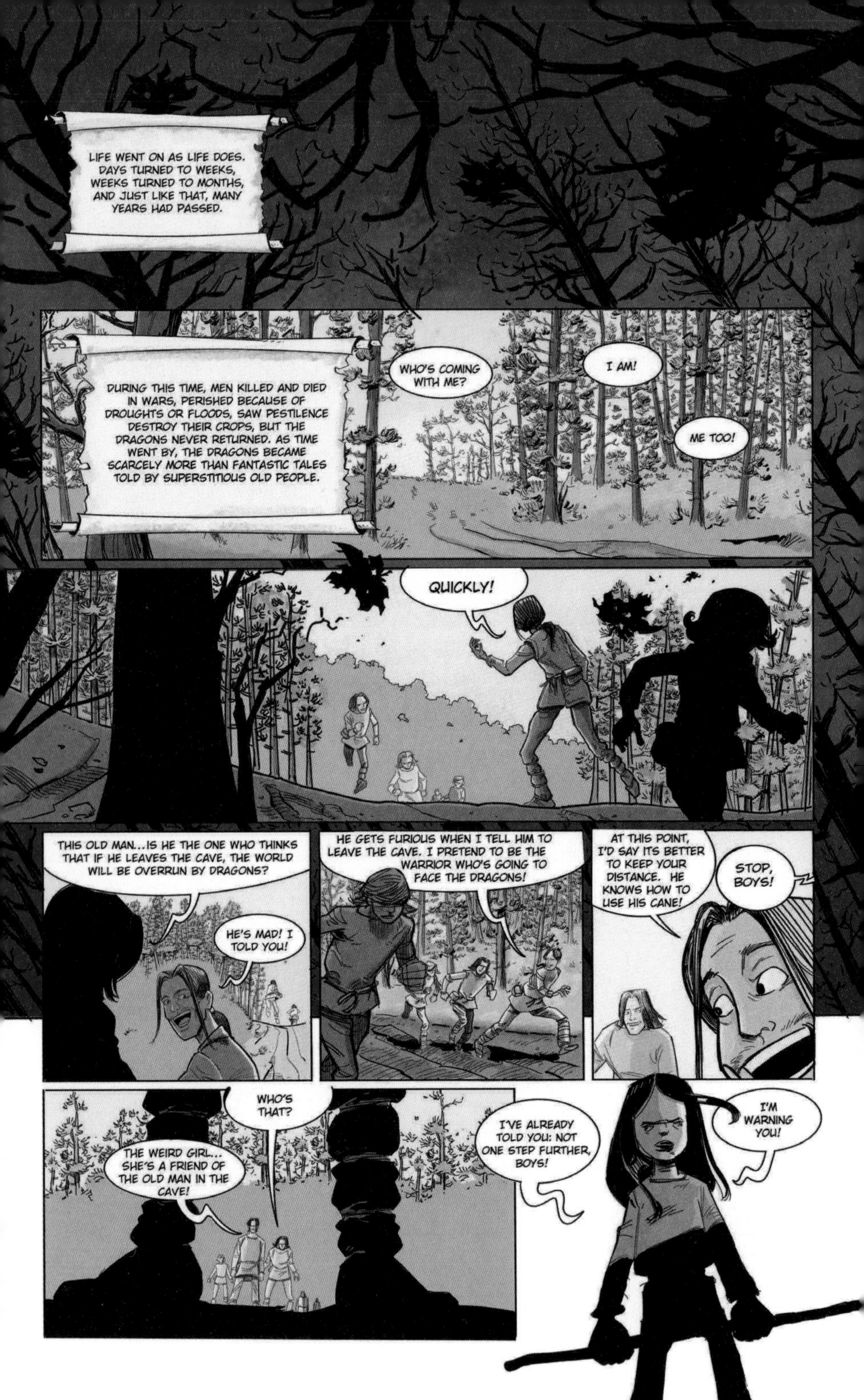

LIFE WENT ON AS LIFE DOES. DAYS TURNED TO WEEKS, WEEKS TURNED TO MONTHS, AND JUST LIKE THAT, MANY YEARS HAD PASSED.
DURING THIS TIME, MEN KILLED AND DIED IN WARS, PERISHED BECAUSE OF DROUGHTS OR FLOODS, SAW PESTILENCE DESTROY THEIR CROPS, BUT THE DRAGONS NEVER RETURNED. AS TIME WENT BY, THE DRAGONS BECAME SCARCELY MORE THAN FANTASTIC TALES TOLD BY SUPERSTITIOUS OLD PEOPLE.
WHO'S COMING WITH ME?
I AM!
ME TOO!
QUICKLY!
THIS OLD MAN...IS HE THE ONE WHO THINKS THAT IF HE LEAVES THE CAVE, THE WORLD WILL BE OVERRUN BY DRAGONS?
HE'S MAD! I TOLD YOU!
HE GETS FURIOUS WHEN I TELL HIM TO LEAVE THE CAVE. I PRETEND TO BE THE WARRIOR WHO'S GOING TO FACE THE DRAGONS!
AT THIS POINT, I'D SAY ITS BETTER TO KEEP YOUR DISTANCE. HE KNOWS HOW TO USE HIS CANE!
STOP, BOYS!
WHO'S THAT?
THE WEIRD GIRL... SHE'S A FRIEND OF THE OLD MAN IN THE CAVE!
I'VE ALREADY TOLD YOU: NOT ONE STEP FURTHER, BOYS!
I'M WARNING YOU!

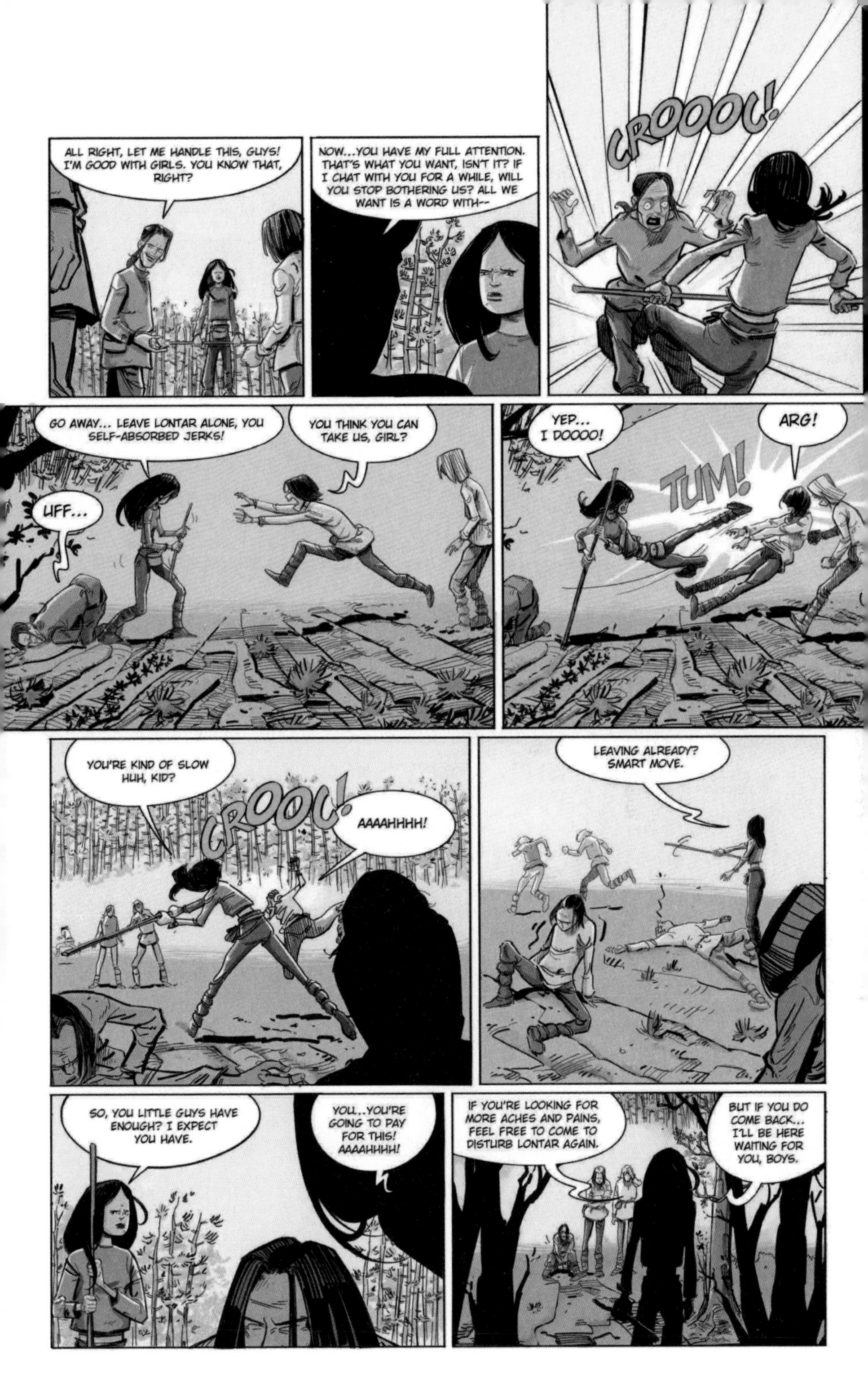
ALL RIGHT, LET ME HANDLE THIS, GUYS! I'M GOOD WITH GIRLS. YOU KNOW THAT, RIGHT?
NOW...YOU HAVE MY FULL ATTENTION. THAT'S WHAT YOU WANT, ISN'T IT? IF I CHAT WITH YOU FOR A WHILE, WILL YOU STOP BOTHERING US? ALL WE WANT IS A WORD WITH--
CROOOC!
GO AWAY... LEAVE LONTAR ALONE, YOU SELF-ABSORBED JERKS!
UFF...
YOU THINK YOU CAN TAKE US, GIRL?
YEP... I DOOOO!
TUM!
ARG!
YOU'RE KIND OF SLOW HUH, KID?
CROOC!
AAAAHHHH!
LEAVING ALREADY? SMART MOVE.
SO, YOU LITTLE GUYS HAVE ENOUGH? I EXPECT YOU HAVE.
YOU...YOU'RE GOING TO PAY FOR THIS! AAAAHHHH!
IF YOU'RE LOOKING FOR MORE ACHES AND PAINS, FEEL FREE TO COME TO DISTURB LONTAR AGAIN.
BUT IF YOU DO COME BACK... I'LL BE HERE WAITING FOR YOU, BOYS.

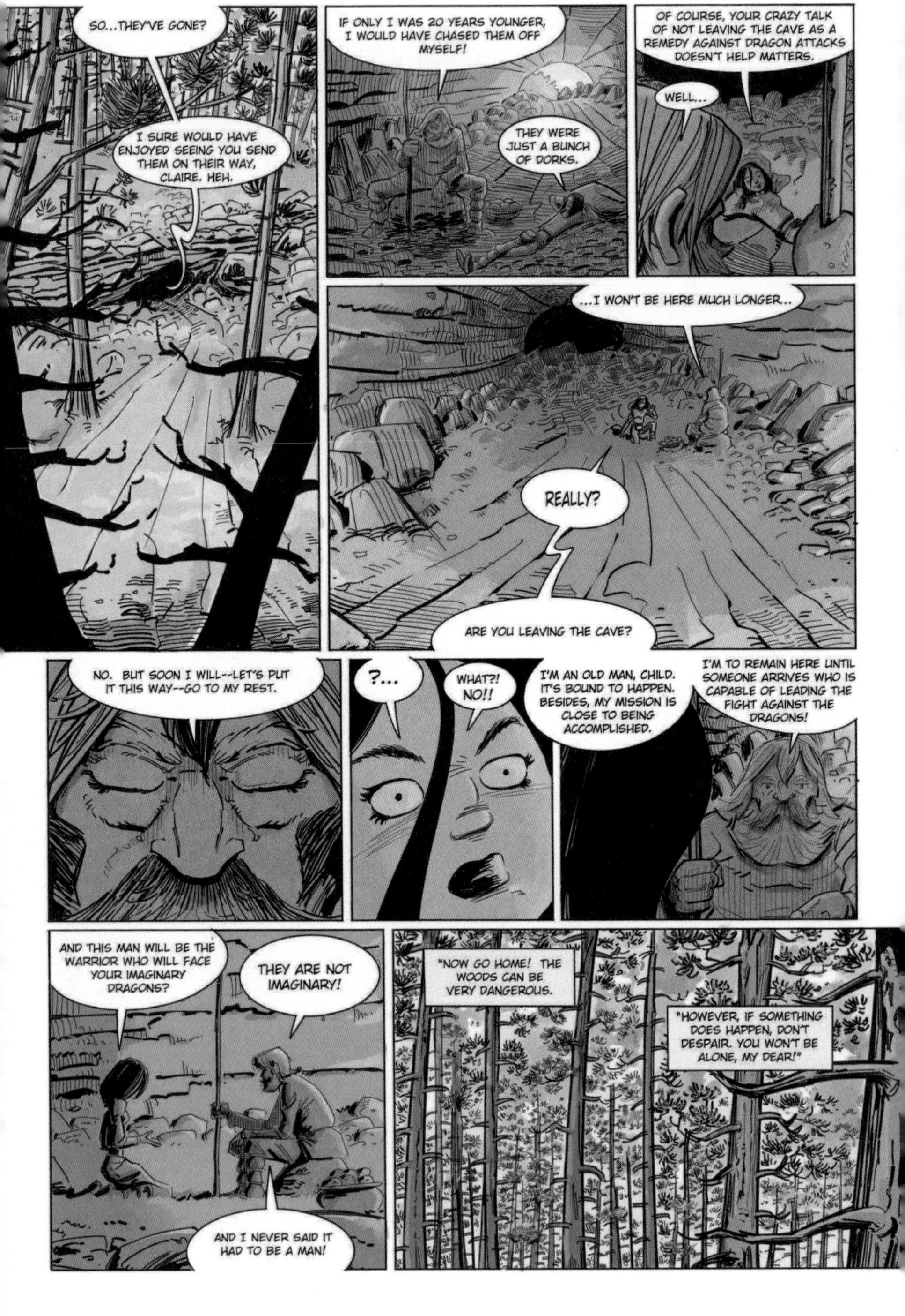
SO...THEY'VE GONE?
I SURE WOULD HAVE ENJOYED SEEING YOU SEND THEM ON THEIR WAY, CLAIRE. HEH.
IF ONLY I WAS 20 YEARS YOUNGER, I WOULD HAVE CHASED THEM OFF MYSELF!
THEY WERE JUST A BUNCH OF DORKS.
OF COURSE, YOUR CRAZY TALK OF NOT LEAVING THE CAVE AS A REMEDY AGAINST DRAGON ATTACKS DOESN'T HELP MATTERS.
WELL...
...I WON'T BE HERE MUCH LONGER...
REALLY?
ARE YOU LEAVING THE CAVE?
NO. BUT SOON I WILL--LET'S PUT IT THIS WAY--GO TO MY REST.
?...
WHAT?! NO!!
I'M AN OLD MAN, CHILD. IT'S BOUND TO HAPPEN. BESIDES, MY MISSION IS CLOSE TO BEING ACCOMPLISHED.
I'M TO REMAIN HERE UNTIL SOMEONE ARRIVES WHO IS CAPABLE OF LEADING THE FIGHT AGAINST THE DRAGONS!
AND THIS MAN WILL BE THE WARRIOR WHO WILL FACE YOUR IMAGINARY DRAGONS?
THEY ARE NOT IMAGINARY!
AND I NEVER SAID IT HAD TO BE A MAN!
"NOW GO HOME! THE WOODS CAN BE VERY DANGEROUS.
"HOWEVER, IF SOMETHING DOES HAPPEN, DON'T DESPAIR. YOU WON'T BE ALONE, MY DEAR!"

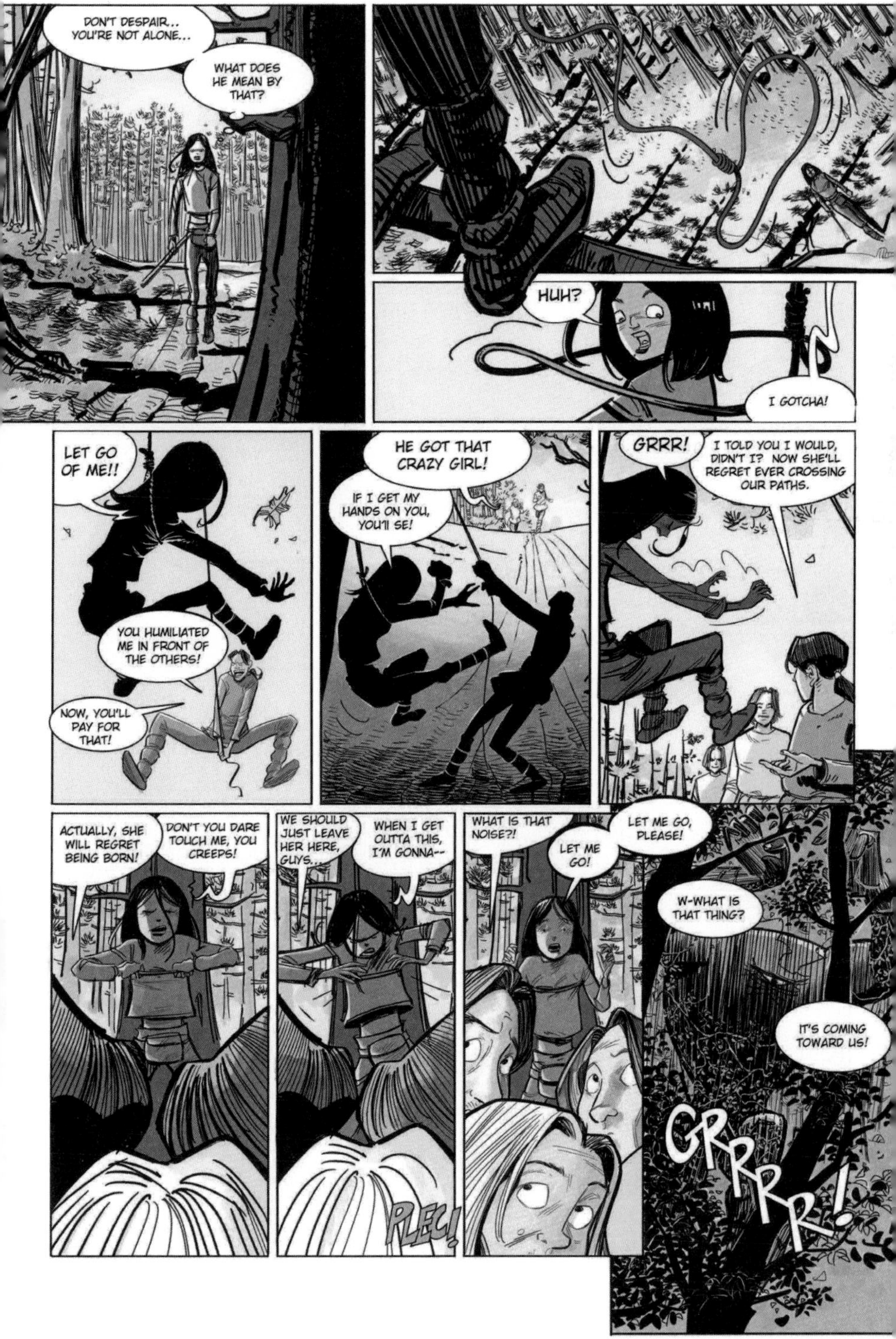
DON'T DESPAIR... YOU'RE NOT ALONE...
WHAT DOES HE MEAN BY THAT?
HUH?
I GOTCHA!
LET GO OF ME!!
YOU HUMILIATED ME IN FRONT OF THE OTHERS!
NOW, YOU'LL PAY FOR THAT!
HE GOT THAT CRAZY GIRL!
IF I GET MY HANDS ON YOU, YOU'll SE!
GRRR!
I TOLD YOU I WOULD, DIDN'T I? NOW SHE'LL REGRET EVER CROSSING OUR PATHS.
ACTUALLY, SHE WILL REGRET BEING BORN!
DON'T YOU DARE TOUCH ME, YOU CREEPS!
WE SHOULD JUST LEAVE HER HERE, GUYS...
WHEN I GET OUTTA THIS, I'M GONNA--
PLEC!
WHAT IS THAT NOISE?!
LET ME GO!
LET ME GO, PLEASE!
W-WHAT IS THAT THING?
IT'S COMING TOWARD US!
GRRRRR!

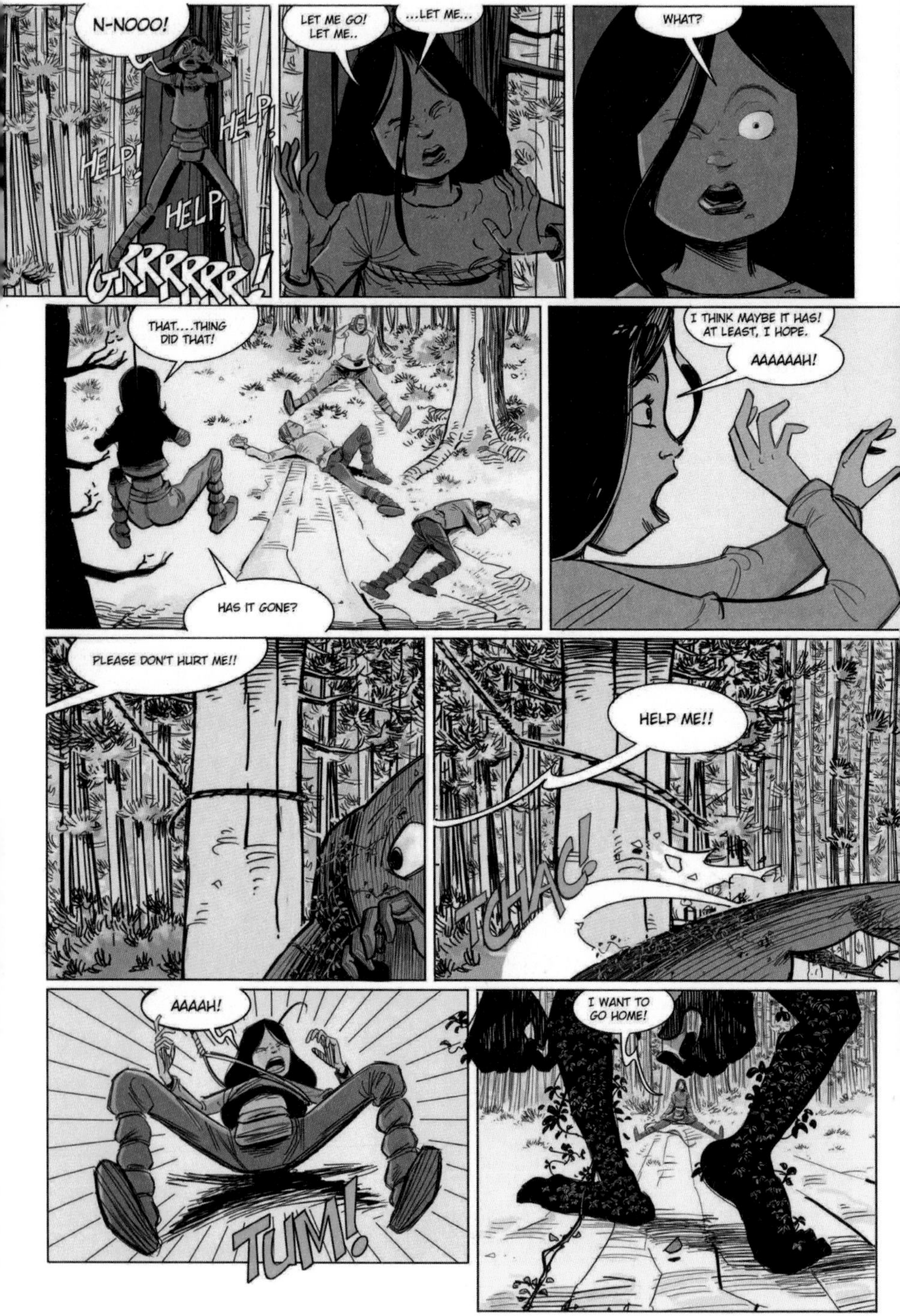
N-NOOO!
HELP!
HELP!
HELP!
GRRRRRR!
LET ME GO! LET ME..
...LET ME...
WHAT?
THAT....THING DID THAT!
HAS IT GONE?
I THINK MAYBE IT HAS! AT LEAST, I HOPE.
AAAAAAH!
PLEASE DON'T HURT ME!!
HELP ME!!
TCHAC!
AAAAH!
TUM!
I WANT TO GO HOME!

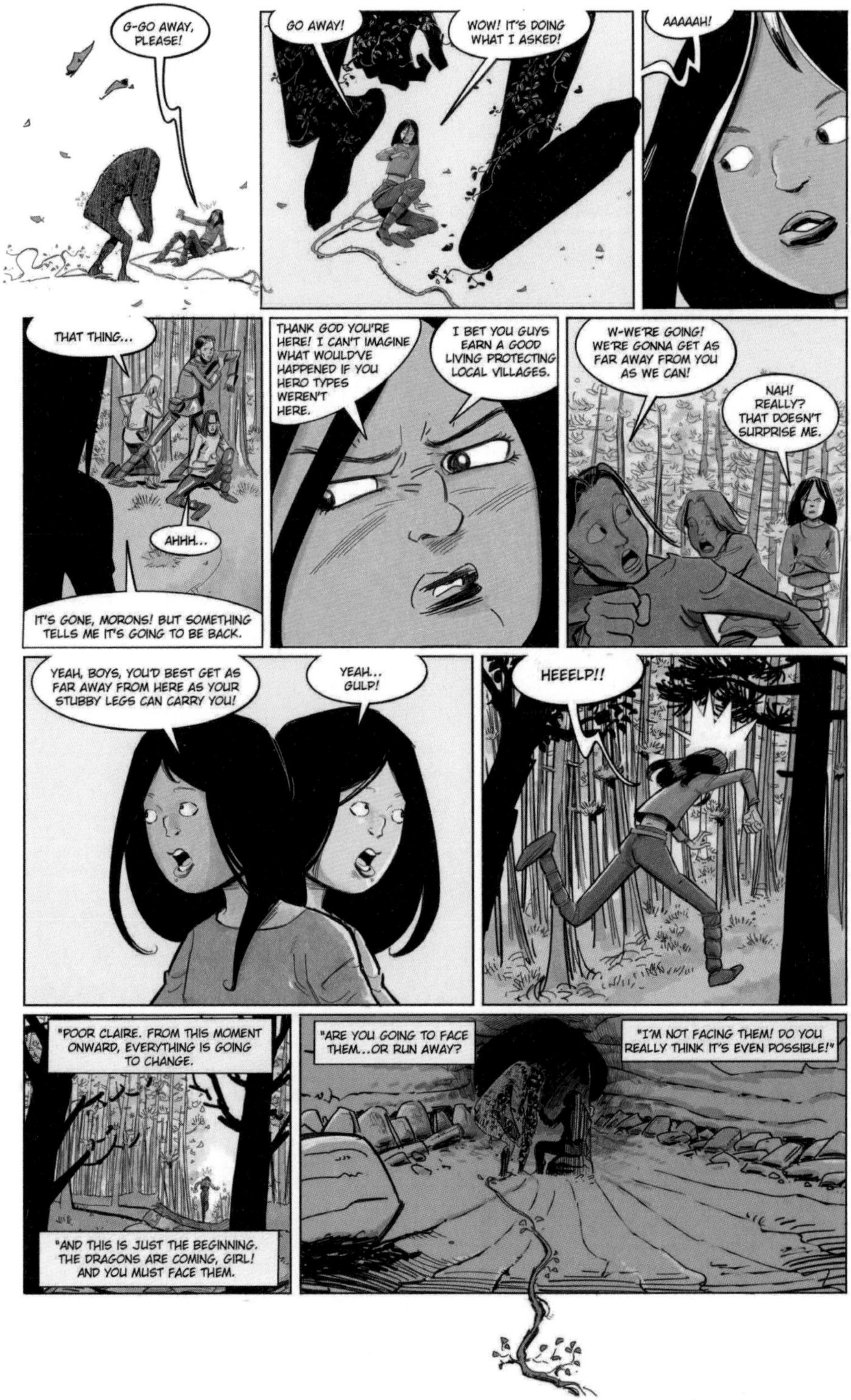
G-GO AWAY, PLEASE!
GO AWAY!
WOW! IT'S DOING WHAT I ASKED!
AAAAAH!
THAT THING...
AHHH...
IT'S GONE, MORONS! BUT SOMETHING TELLS ME IT'S GOING TO BE BACK.
THANK GOD YOU'RE HERE! I CAN'T IMAGINE WHAT WOULD'VE HAPPENED IF YOU HERO TYPES WEREN'T HERE.
I BET YOU GUYS EARN A GOOD LIVING PROTECTING LOCAL VILLAGES.
W-WE'RE GOING! WE'RE GONNA GET AS FAR AWAY FROM YOU AS WE CAN!
NAH! REALLY? THAT DOESN'T SURPRISE ME.
YEAH, BOYS, YOU'D BEST GET AS FAR AWAY FROM HERE AS YOUR STUBBY LEGS CAN CARRY YOU!
YEAH... GULP!
HEEELP!!
"POOR CLAIRE. FROM THIS MOMENT ONWARD, EVERYTHING IS GOING TO CHANGE.
"AND THIS IS JUST THE BEGINNING. THE DRAGONS ARE COMING, GIRL! AND YOU MUST FACE THEM.
"ARE YOU GOING TO FACE THEM...OR RUN AWAY?
"I'M NOT FACING THEM! DO YOU REALLY THINK IT'S EVEN POSSIBLE!"

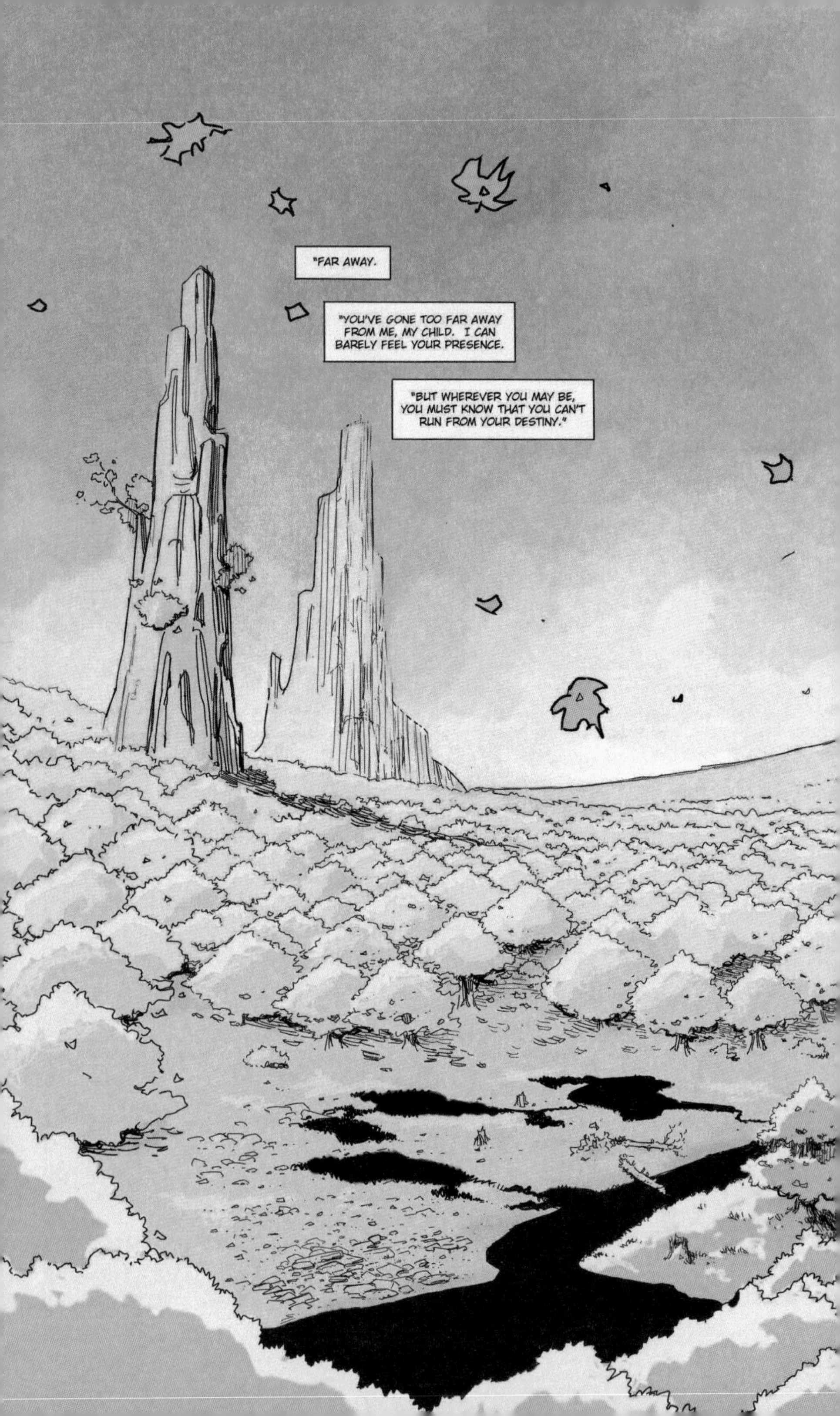
"FAR AWAY.
"YOU'VE GONE TOO FAR AWAY FROM ME, MY CHILD. I CAN BARELY FEEL YOUR PRESENCE.
"BUT WHEREVER YOU MAY BE, YOU MUST KNOW THAT YOU CAN'T RUN FROM YOUR DESTINY."

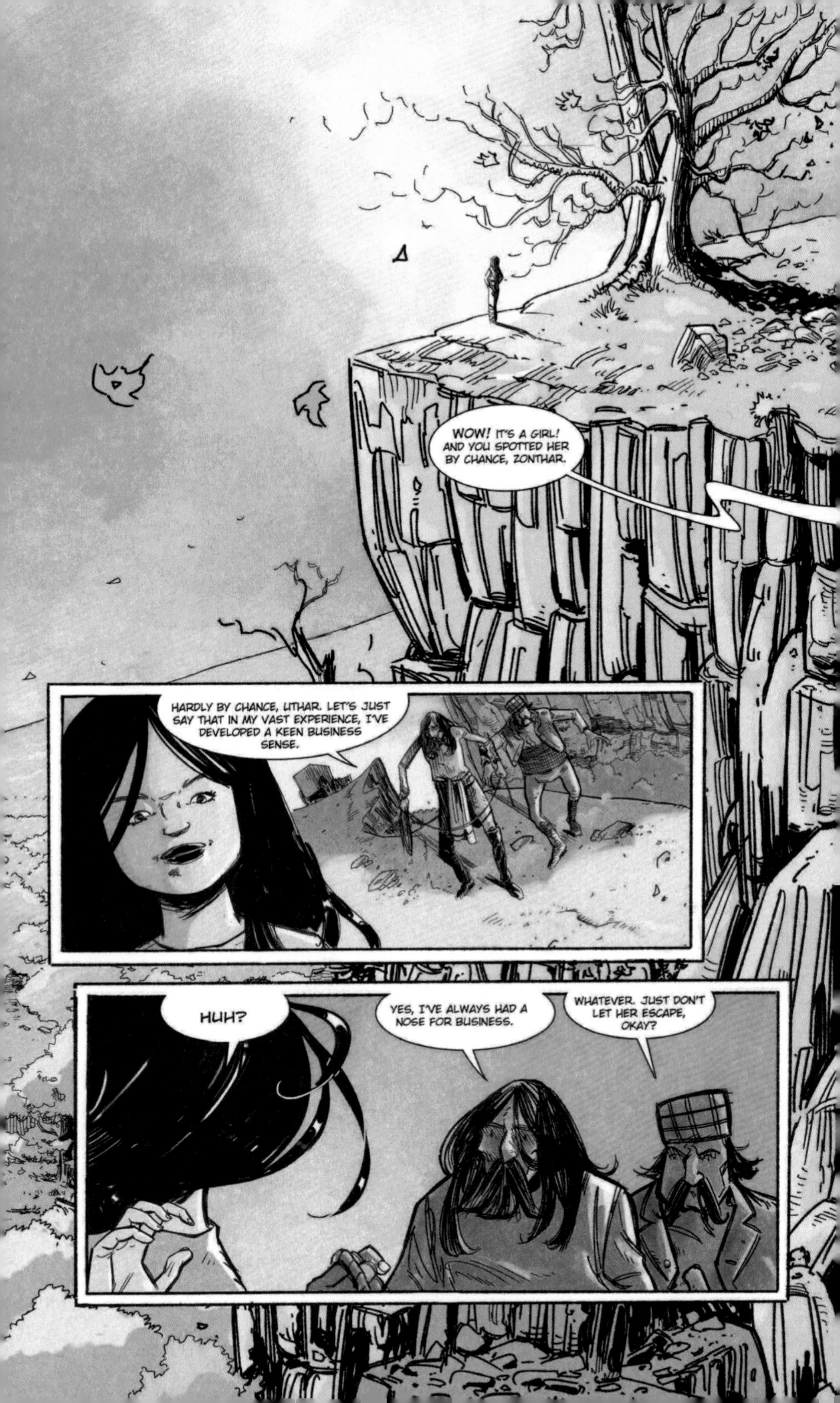
WOW! IT'S A GIRL! AND YOU SPOTTED HER BY CHANCE, ZONTHAR.
HARDLY BY CHANCE, UTHAR. LET'S JUST SAY THAT IN MY VAST EXPERIENCE, I'VE DEVELOPED A KEEN BUSINESS SENSE.
HUH?
YES, I'VE ALWAYS HAD A NOSE FOR BUSINESS.
WHATEVER. JUST DON'T LET HER ESCAPE, OKAY?

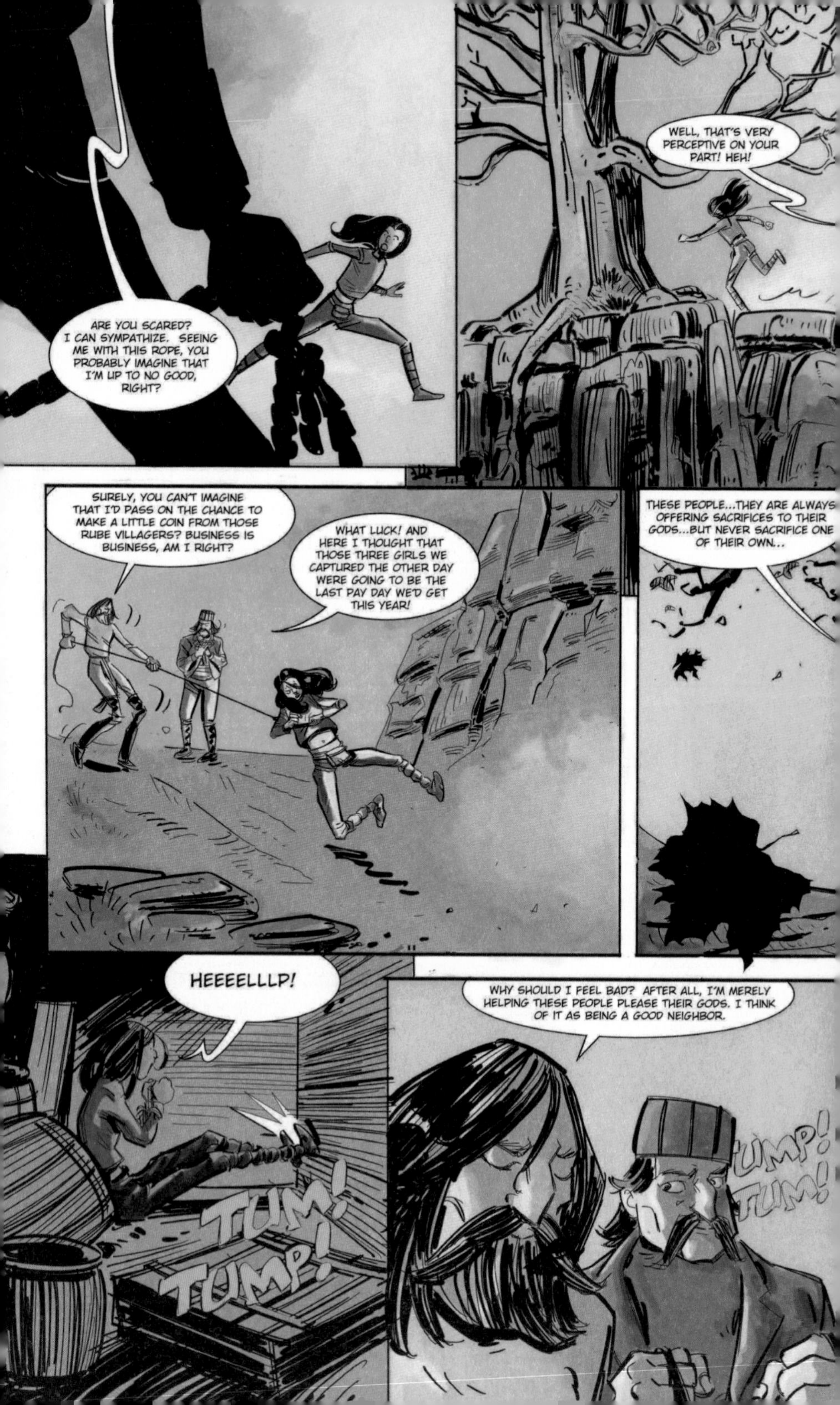
ARE YOU SCARED? I CAN SYMPATHIZE. SEEING ME WITH THIS ROPE, YOU PROBABLY IMAGINE THAT I'M UP TO NO GOOD, RIGHT?
WELL, THAT'S VERY PERCEPTIVE ON YOUR PART! HEH!
SURELY, YOU CAN'T IMAGINE THAT I'D PASS ON THE CHANCE TO MAKE A LITTLE COIN FROM THOSE RUBE VILLAGERS? BUSINESS IS BUSINESS, AM I RIGHT?
WHAT LUCK! AND HERE I THOUGHT THAT THOSE THREE GIRLS WE CAPTURED THE OTHER DAY WERE GOING TO BE THE LAST PAY DAY WE'D GET THIS YEAR!
THESE PEOPLE...THEY ARE ALWAYS OFFERING SACRIFICES TO THEIR GODS...BUT NEVER SACRIFICE ONE OF THEIR OWN...
HEEEELLLP!
TUMP! TUMP!
WHY SHOULD I FEEL BAD? AFTER ALL, I'M MERELY HELPING THESE PEOPLE PLEASE THEIR GODS. I THINK OF IT AS BEING A GOOD NEIGHBOR.
TUMP! TUMP!

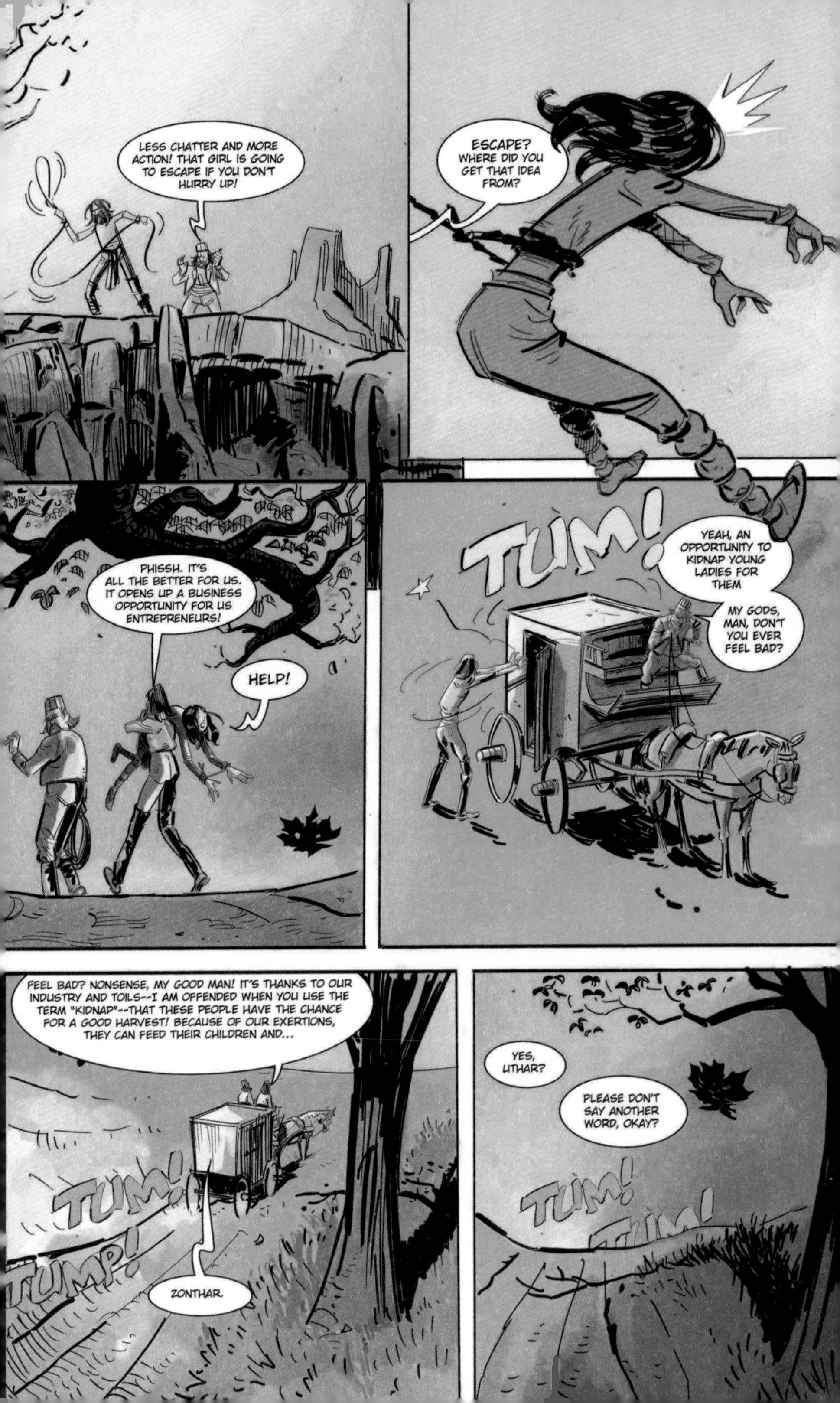
LESS CHATTER AND MORE ACTION! THAT GIRL IS GOING TO ESCAPE IF YOU DON'T HURRY UP!
ESCAPE? WHERE DID YOU GET THAT IDEA FROM?
PHISSH. IT'S ALL THE BETTER FOR US. IT OPENS UP A BUSINESS OPPORTUNITY FOR US ENTREPRENEURS!
HELP!
TUM!
YEAH, AN OPPORTUNITY TO KIDNAP YOUNG LADIES FOR THEM
MY GODS, MAN, DON'T YOU EVER FEEL BAD?
FEEL BAD? NONSENSE, MY GOOD MAN! IT'S THANKS TO OUR INDUSTRY AND TOILS--I AM OFFENDED WHEN YOU USE THE TERM "KIDNAP"--THAT THESE PEOPLE HAVE THE CHANCE FOR A GOOD HARVEST! BECAUSE OF OUR EXERTIONS, THEY CAN FEED THEIR CHILDREN AND...
TUM!
TUMP!
ZONTHAR.
YES, UTHAR?
PLEASE DON'T SAY ANOTHER WORD, OKAY?
TUM!
TUM!

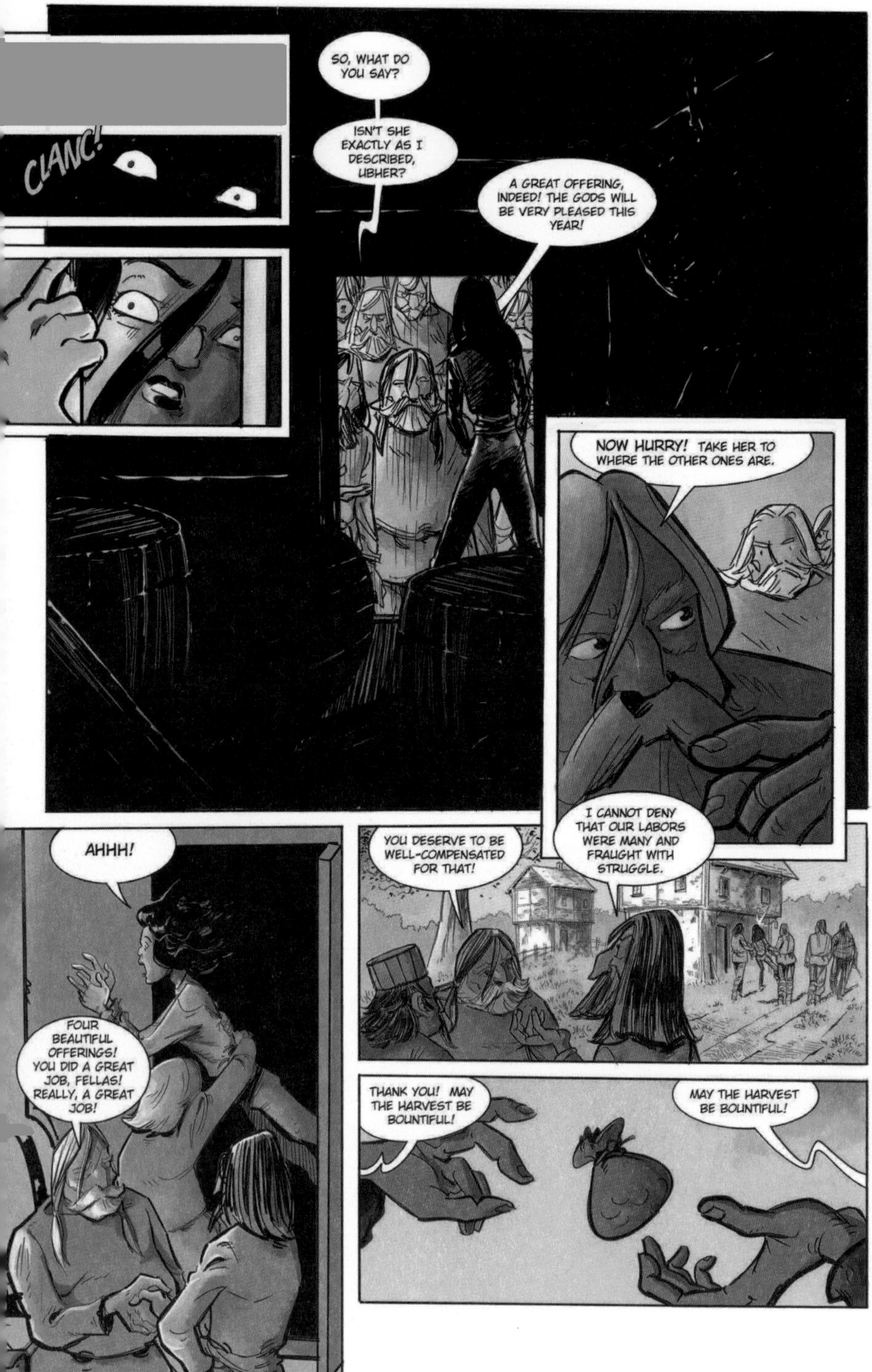
CLANC!
SO, WHAT DO YOU SAY?
ISN'T SHE EXACTLY AS I DESCRIBED, UBHER?
A GREAT OFFERING, INDEED! THE GODS WILL BE VERY PLEASED THIS YEAR!
NOW HURRY! TAKE HER TO WHERE THE OTHER ONES ARE.
AHHH!
FOUR BEAUTIFUL OFFERINGS! YOU DID A GREAT JOB, FELLAS! REALLY, A GREAT JOB!
I CANNOT DENY THAT OUR LABORS WERE MANY AND FRAUGHT WITH STRUGGLE.
YOU DESERVE TO BE WELL-COMPENSATED FOR THAT!
THANK YOU! MAY THE HARVEST BE BOUNTIFUL!
MAY THE HARVEST BE BOUNTIFUL!

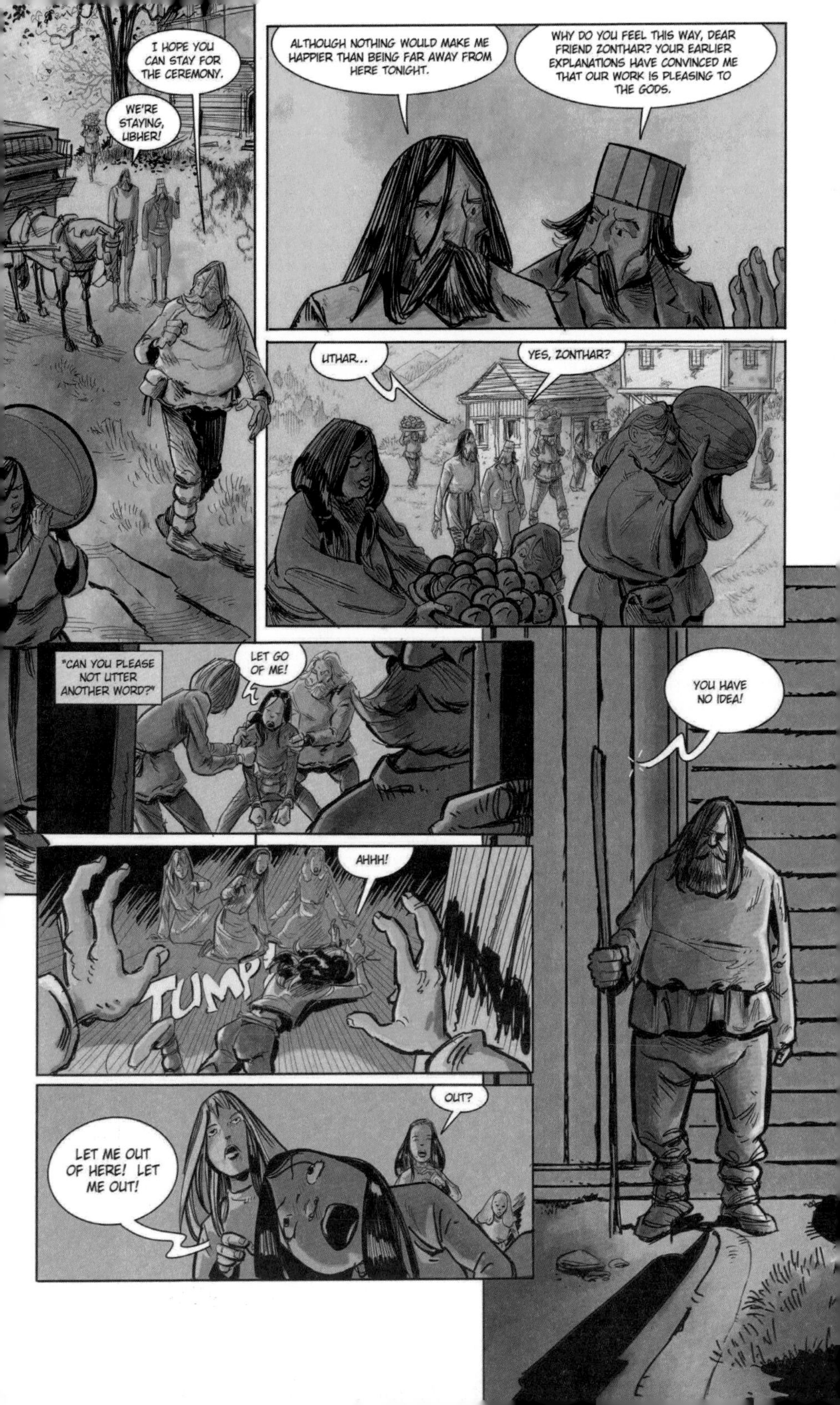
I HOPE YOU CAN STAY FOR THE CEREMONY.
WE'RE STAYING, UBHER!
ALTHOUGH NOTHING WOULD MAKE ME HAPPIER THAN BEING FAR AWAY FROM HERE TONIGHT.
WHY DO YOU FEEL THIS WAY, DEAR FRIEND ZONTHAR? YOUR EARLIER EXPLANATIONS HAVE CONVINCED ME THAT OUR WORK IS PLEASING TO THE GODS.
UTHAR...
YES, ZONTHAR?
"CAN YOU PLEASE NOT UTTER ANOTHER WORD?"
LET GO OF ME!
YOU HAVE NO IDEA!
AHHH!
TUMP!
OUT?
LET ME OUT OF HERE! LET ME OUT!

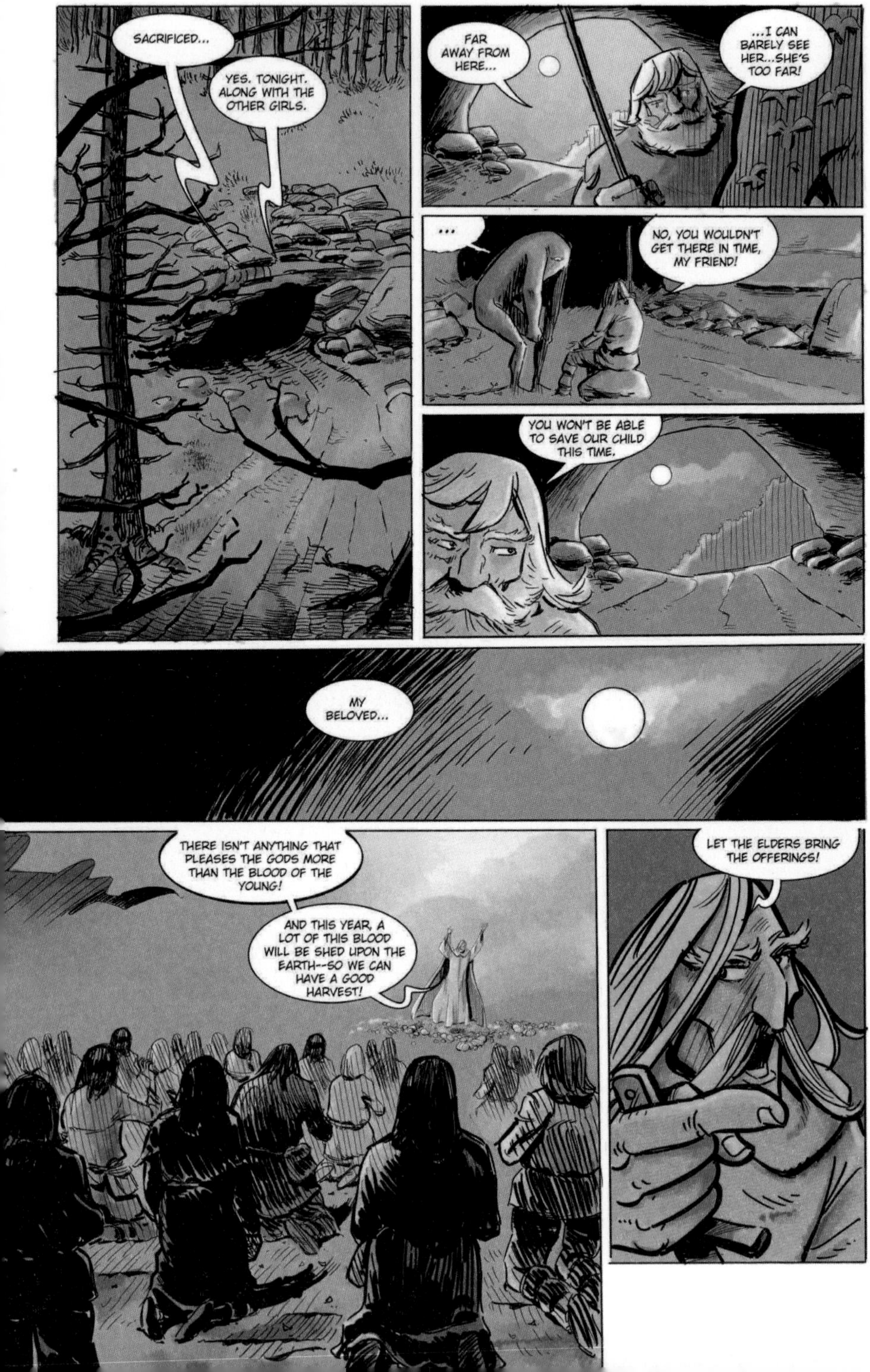
SACRIFICED...
YES. TONIGHT. ALONG WITH THE OTHER GIRLS.
FAR AWAY FROM HERE...
...I CAN BARELY SEE HER...SHE'S TOO FAR!
...
NO, YOU WOULDN'T GET THERE IN TIME, MY FRIEND!
YOU WON'T BE ABLE TO SAVE OUR CHILD THIS TIME.
MY BELOVED...
THERE ISN'T ANYTHING THAT PLEASES THE GODS MORE THAN THE BLOOD OF THE YOUNG!
AND THIS YEAR, A LOT OF THIS BLOOD WILL BE SHED UPON THE EARTH--SO WE CAN HAVE A GOOD HARVEST!
LET THE ELDERS BRING THE OFFERINGS!

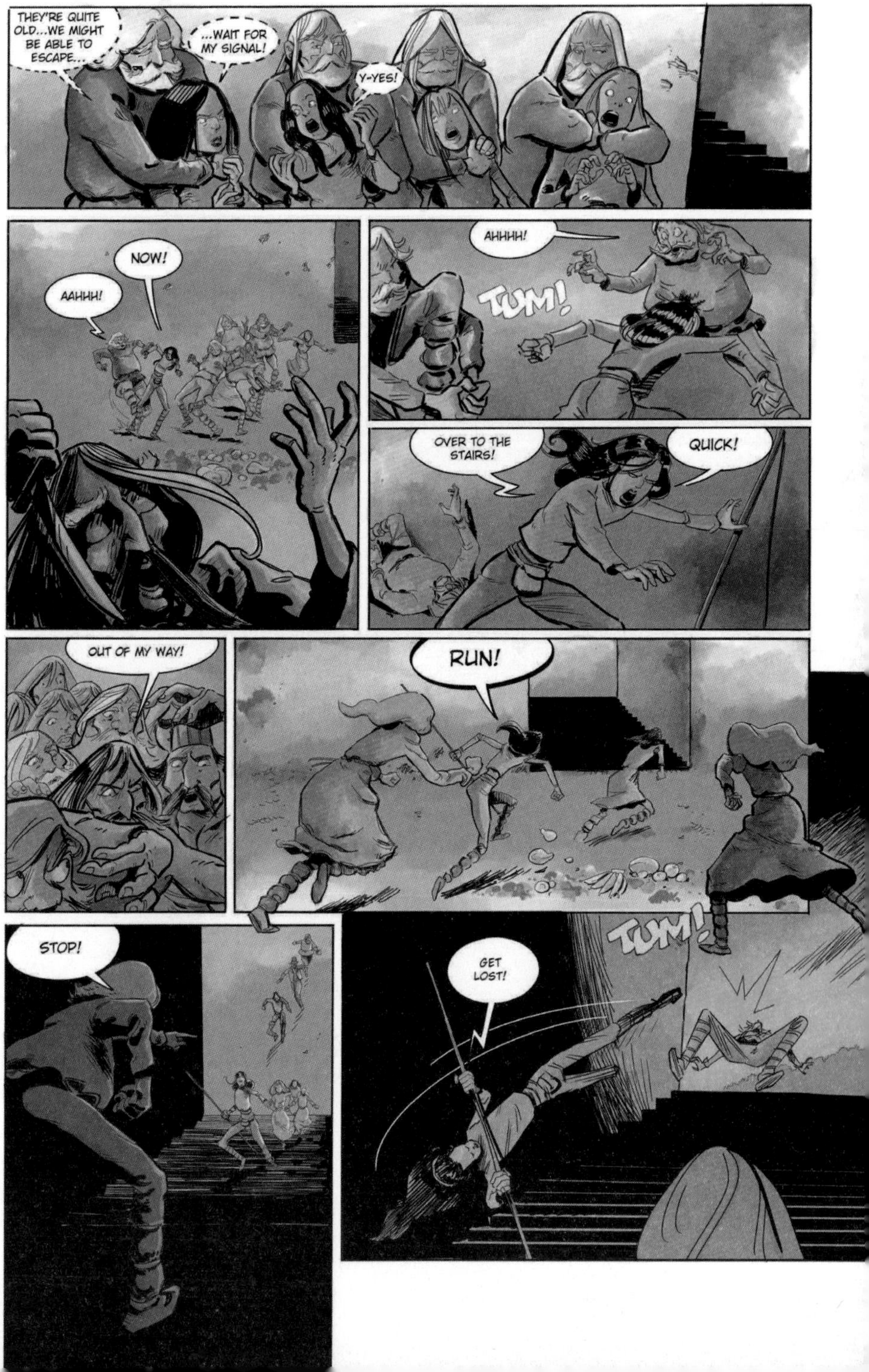
THEY'RE QUITE OLD...WE MIGHT BE ABLE TO ESCAPE...
...WAIT FOR MY SIGNAL!
Y-YES!
NOW!
AAHHH!
AHHHH!
TUM!
OVER TO THE STAIRS!
QUICK!
OUT OF MY WAY!
RUN!
STOP!
TUM!
GET LOST!

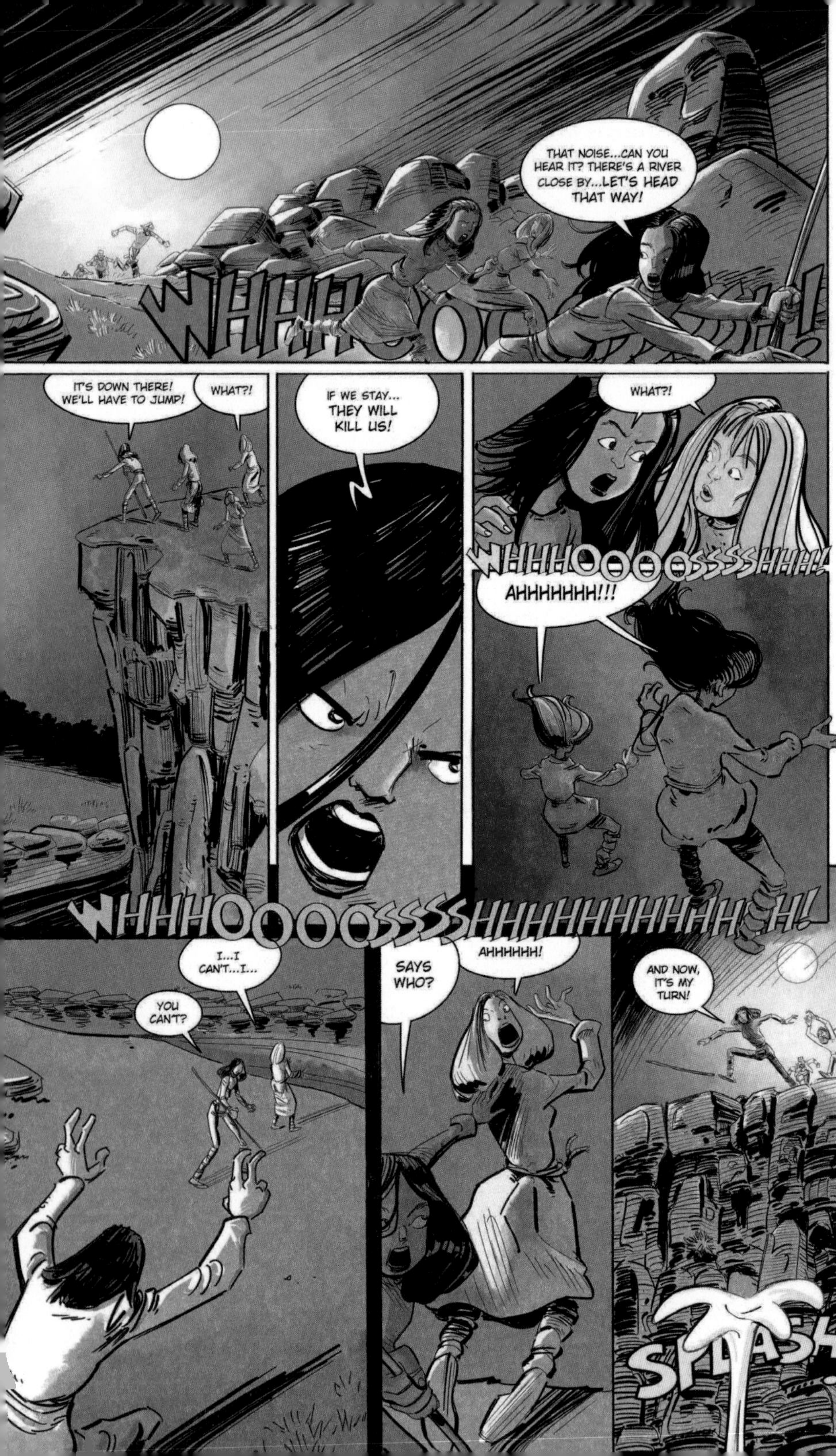
THAT NOISE...CAN YOU HEAR IT? THERE'S A RIVER CLOSE BY...LET'S HEAD THAT WAY!
IT'S DOWN THERE! WE'LL HAVE TO JUMP!
WHAT?!
IF WE STAY... THEY WILL KILL US!
WHAT?!
AHHHHHHH!!!
I...I CAN'T...I...
YOU CAN'T?
SAYS WHO?
AHHHHHH!
AND NOW, IT'S MY TURN!
SPLASH!

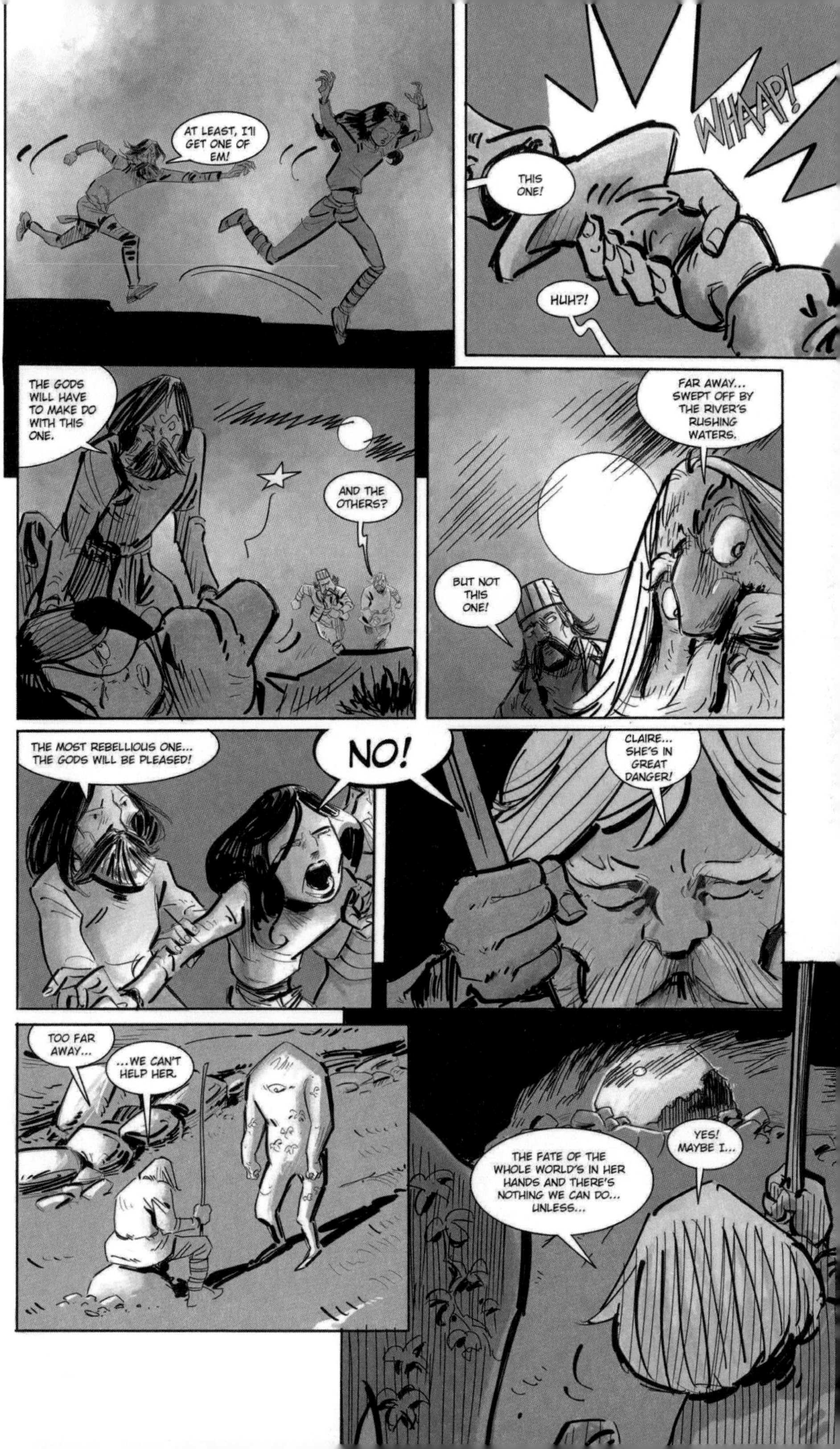
AT LEAST, I'll GET ONE OF EM!
WHAAP!
THIS ONE!
HUH?!
THE GODS WILL HAVE TO MAKE DO WITH THIS ONE.
AND THE OTHERS?
FAR AWAY... SWEPT OFF BY THE RIVER'S RUSHING WATERS.
BUT NOT THIS ONE!
THE MOST REBELLIOUS ONE... THE GODS WILL BE PLEASED!
NO!
CLAIRE... SHE'S IN GREAT DANGER!
TOO FAR AWAY...
...WE CAN'T HELP HER.
THE FATE OF THE WHOLE WORLD'S IN HER HANDS AND THERE'S NOTHING WE CAN DO... UNLESS...
YES! MAYBE I...

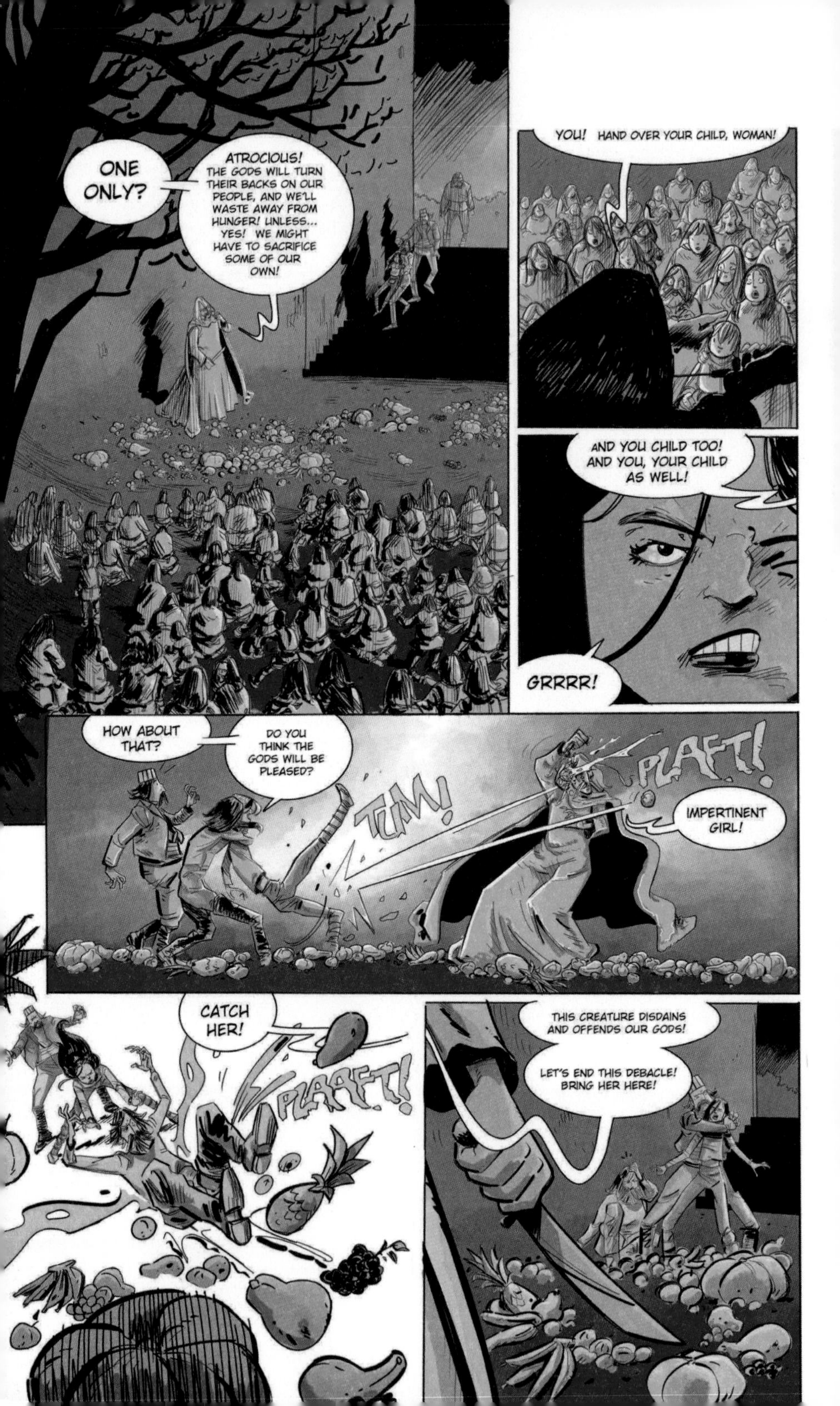
ONE ONLY?
ATROCIOUS! THE GODS WILL TURN THEIR BACKS ON OUR PEOPLE, AND WE'LL WASTE AWAY FROM HUNGER! UNLESS... YES! WE MIGHT HAVE TO SACRIFICE SOME OF OUR OWN!
YOU! HAND OVER YOUR CHILD, WOMAN!
AND YOU CHILD TOO! AND YOU, YOUR CHILD AS WELL!
GRRRR!
HOW ABOUT THAT?
DO YOU THINK THE GODS WILL BE PLEASED?
TUM!
PLAFT!
IMPERTINENT GIRL!
CATCH HER!
PLAAFT!
THIS CREATURE DISDAINS AND OFFENDS OUR GODS!
LET'S END THIS DEBACLE! BRING HER HERE!

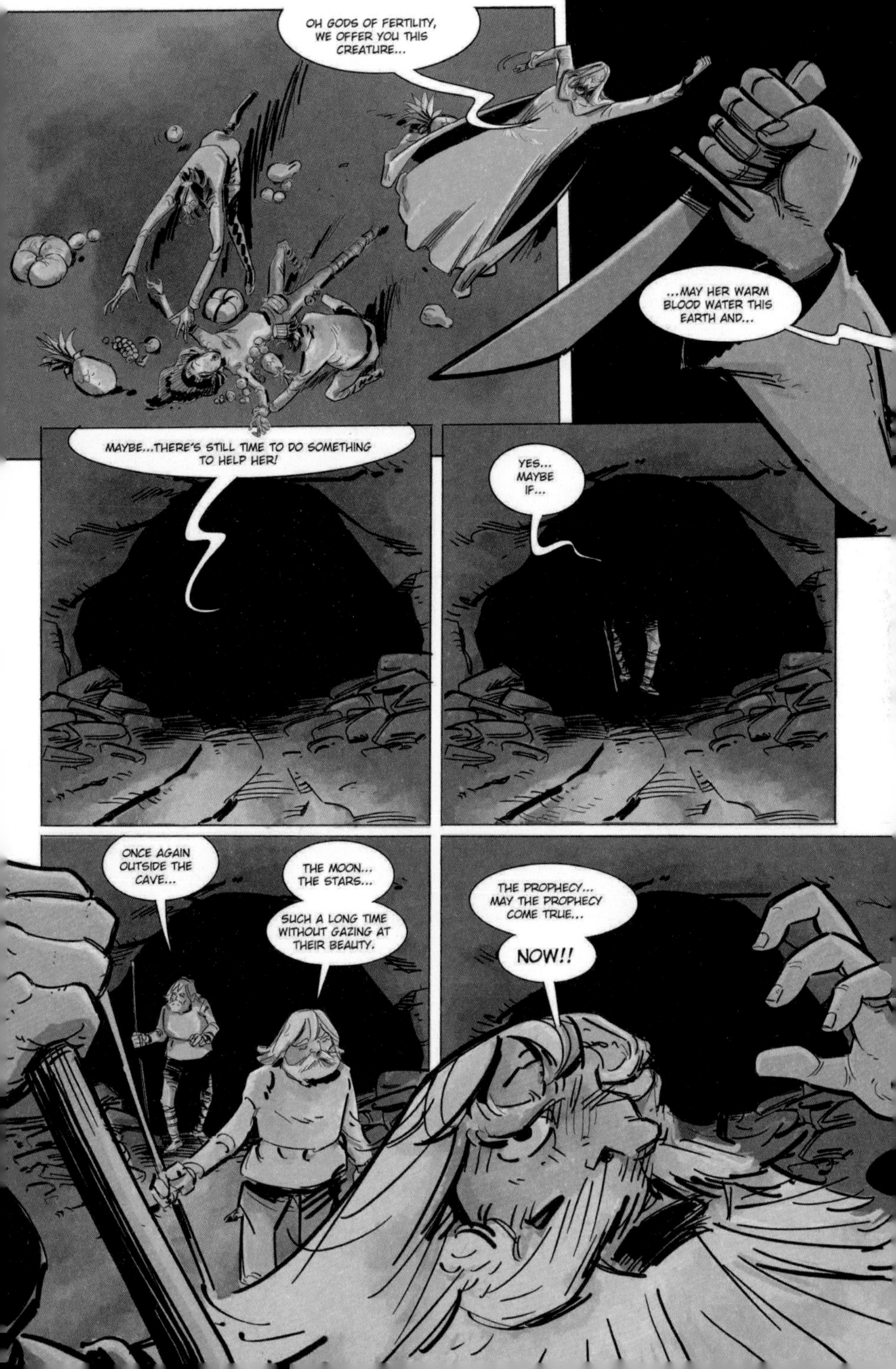
OH GODS OF FERTILITY, WE OFFER YOU THIS CREATURE...
...MAY HER WARM BLOOD WATER THIS EARTH AND...
MAYBE...THERE'S STILL TIME TO DO SOMETHING TO HELP HER!
YES... MAYBE IF...
ONCE AGAIN OUTSIDE THE CAVE...
THE MOON... THE STARS...
SUCH A LONG TIME WITHOUT GAZING AT THEIR BEAUTY.
THE PROPHECY... MAY THE PROPHECY COME TRUE...
NOW!!

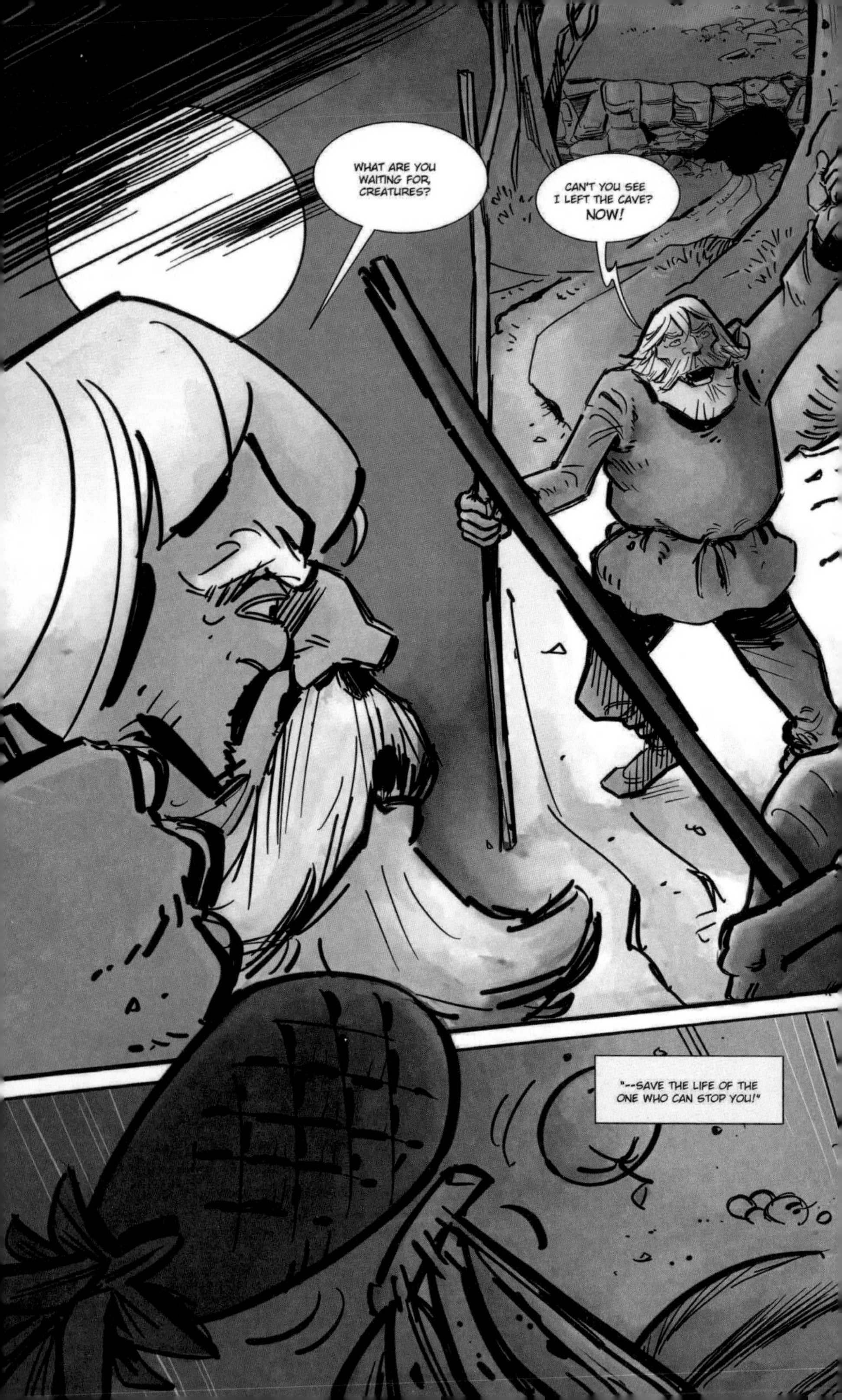
WHAT ARE YOU WAITING FOR, CREATURES?
CAN'T YOU SEE I LEFT THE CAVE? NOW!
"--SAVE THE LIFE OF THE ONE WHO CAN STOP YOU!"

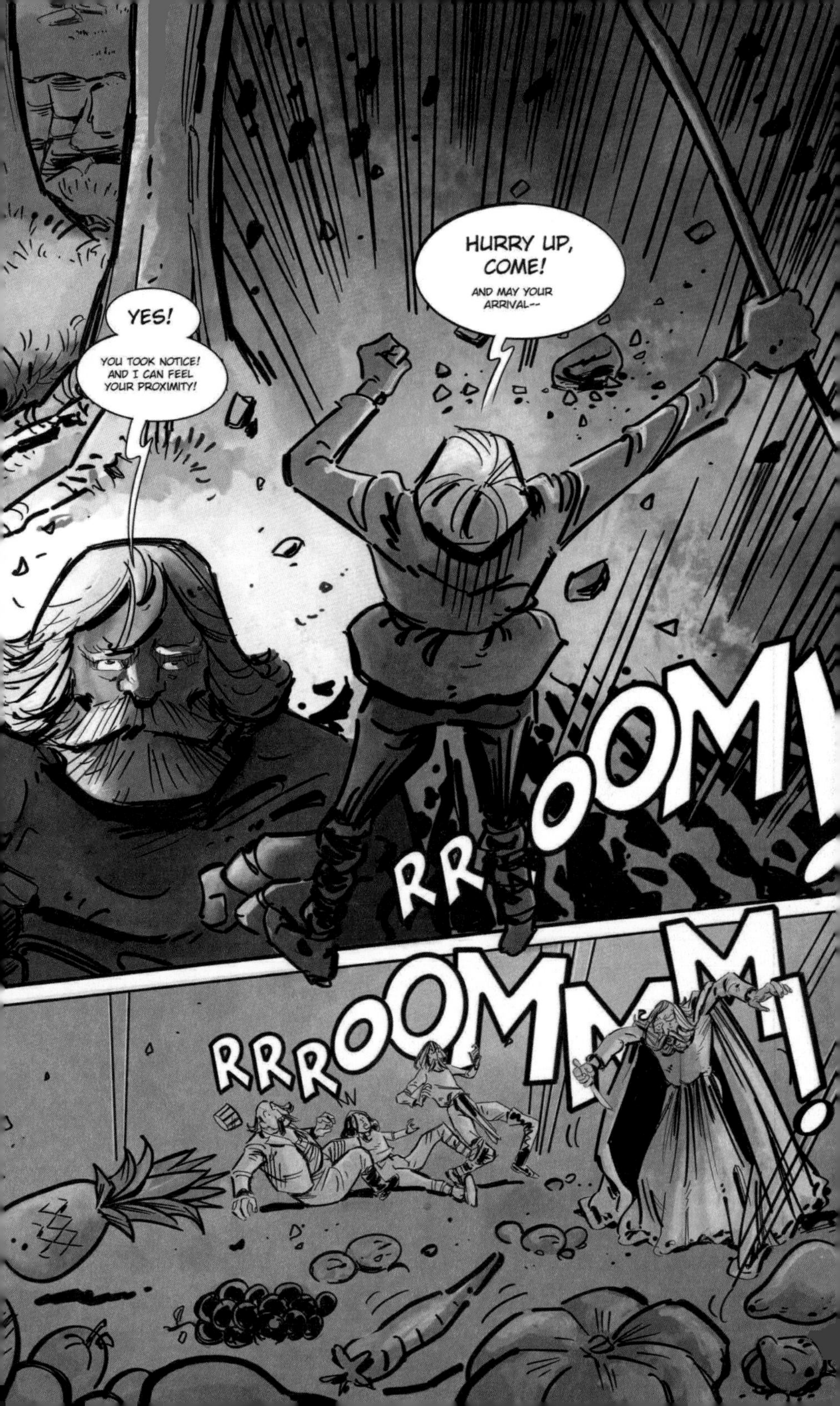
YES!
YOU TOOK NOTICE! AND I CAN FEEL YOUR PROXIMITY!
HURRY UP, COME!
AND MAY YOUR ARRIVAL--
RROOOM!
RRROOOMMM!

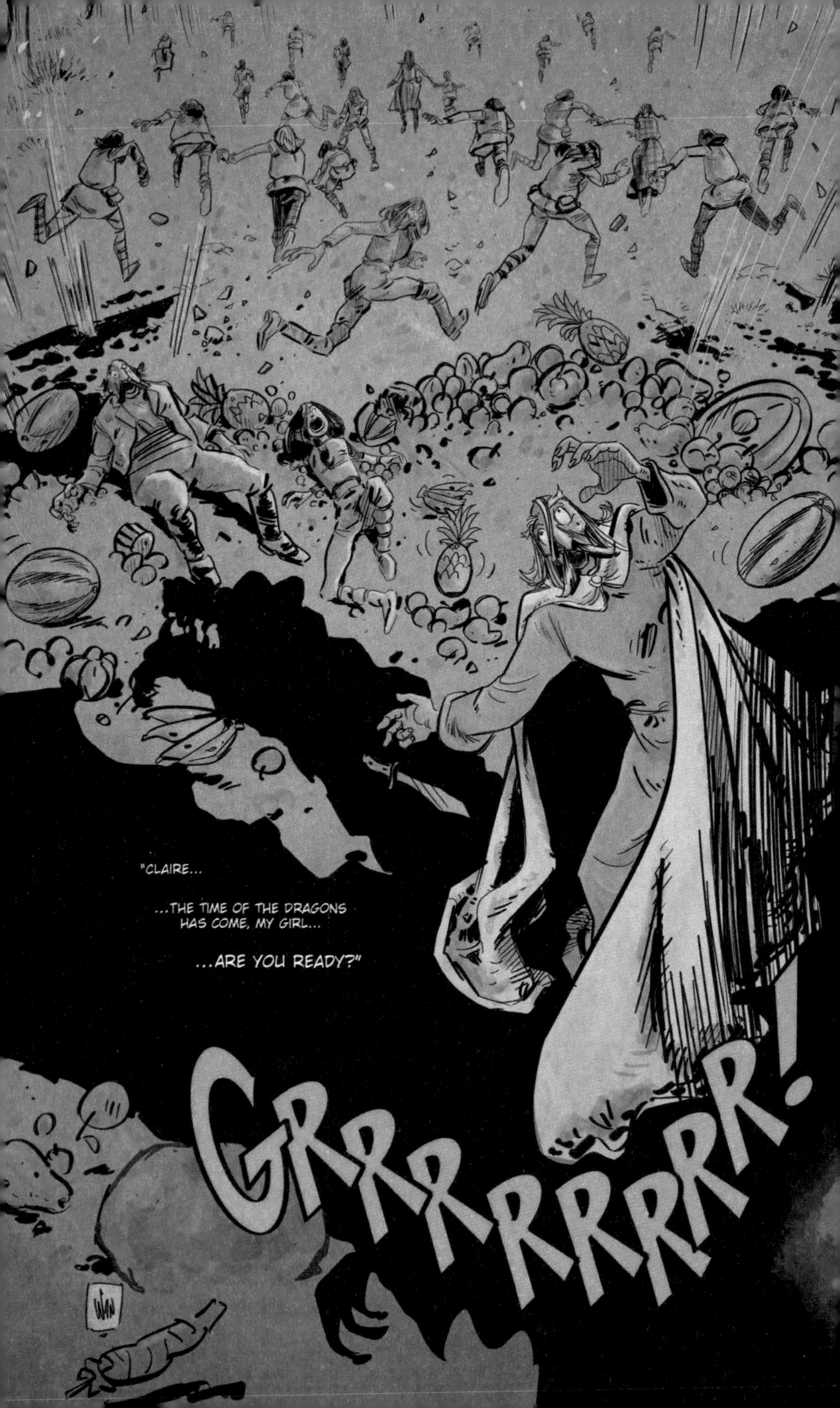
"CLAIRE...
...THE TIME OF THE DRAGONS HAS COME, MY GIRL...
...ARE YOU READY?"
GRRRRRRRR!

CHAPTER 2

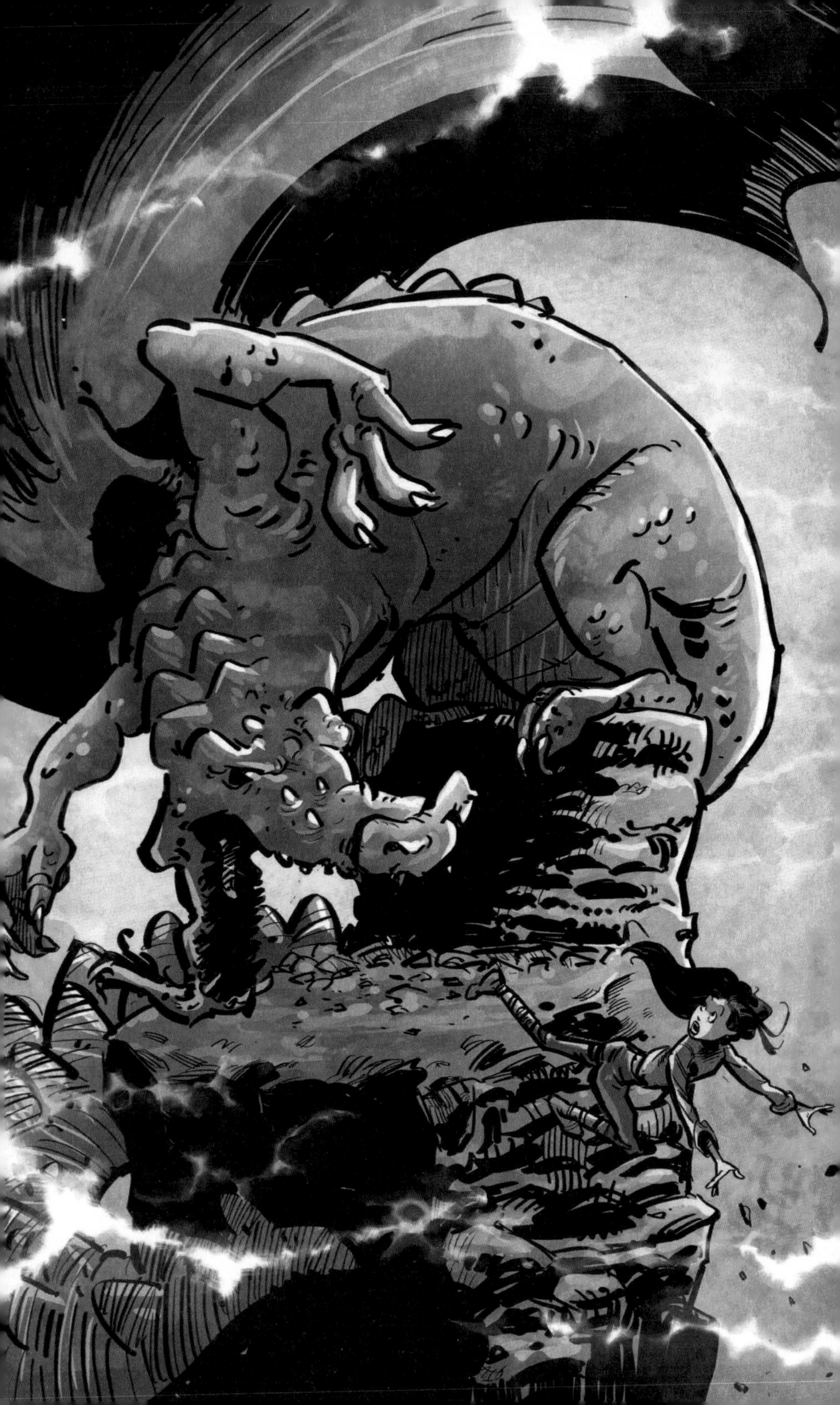

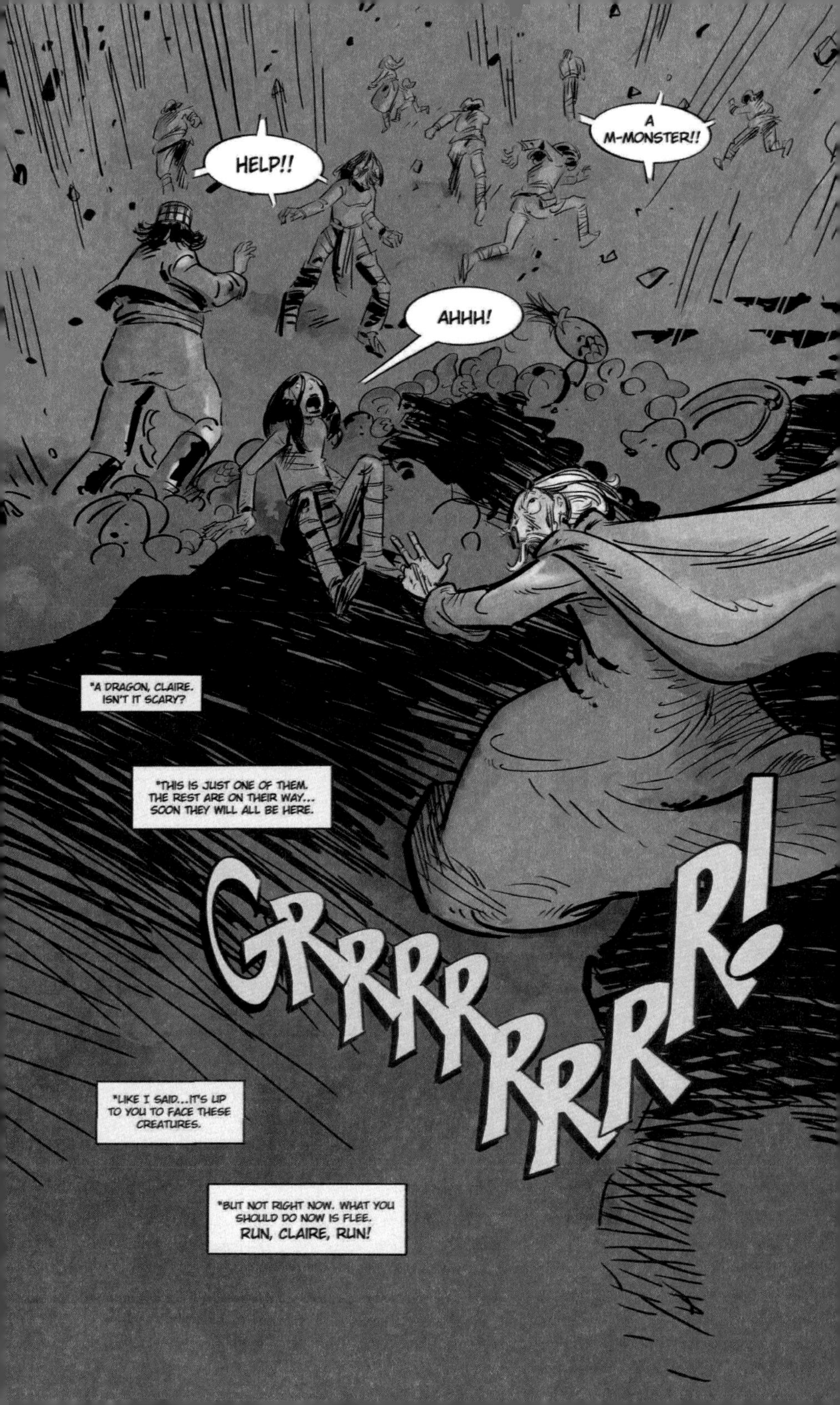
HELP!!
A M-MONSTER!!
AHHH!
*A DRAGON, CLAIRE. ISN'T IT SCARY?
*THIS IS JUST ONE OF THEM. THE REST ARE ON THEIR WAY... SOON THEY WILL ALL BE HERE.
GRRRRRRRR!
*LIKE I SAID...IT'S UP TO YOU TO FACE THESE CREATURES.
*BUT NOT RIGHT NOW. WHAT YOU SHOULD DO NOW IS FLEE. RUN, CLAIRE, RUN!

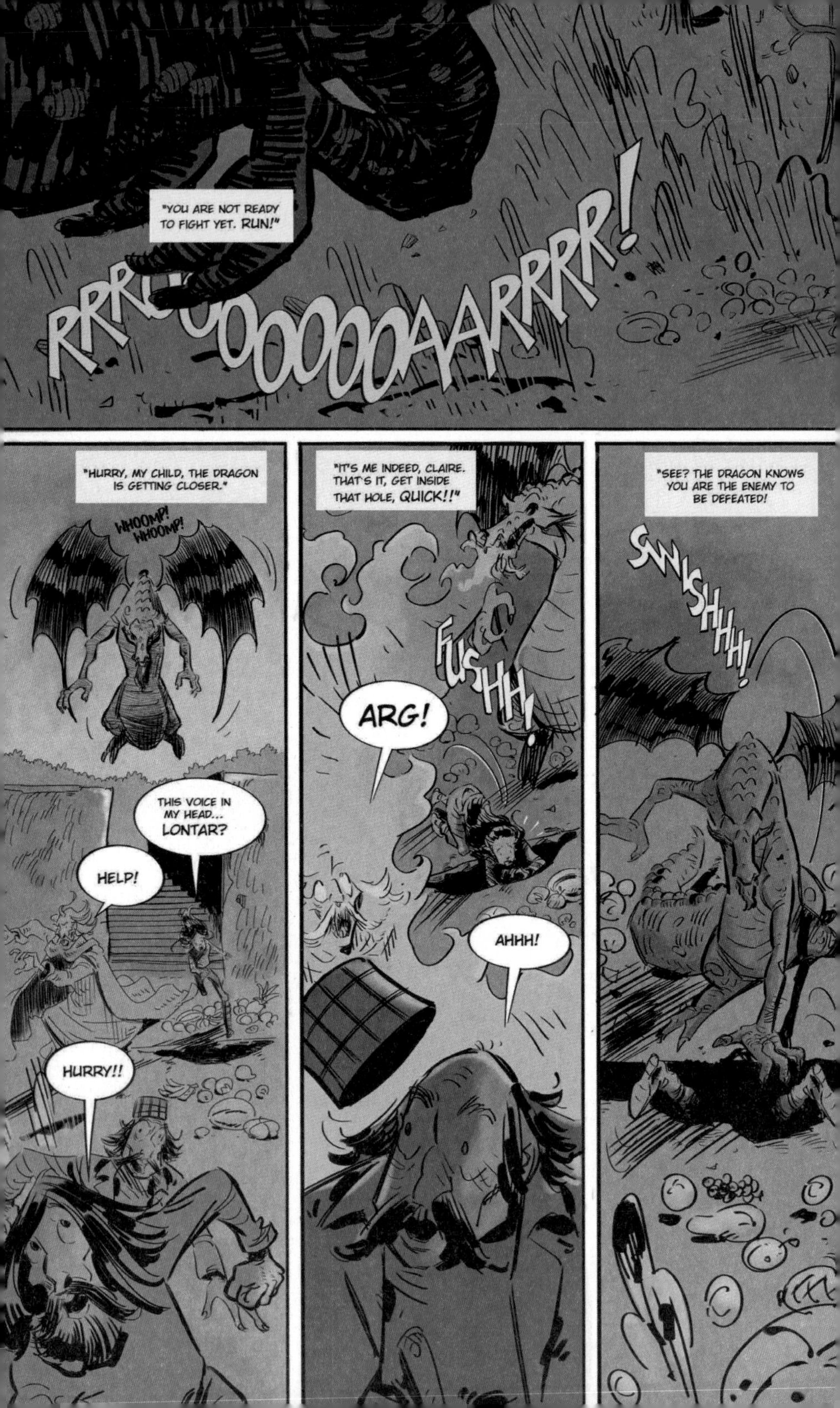

"YOU ARE NOT READY TO FIGHT YET. RUN!"
RRROOOOOOOAARRRR!
"HURRY, MY CHILD, THE DRAGON IS GETTING CLOSER."
WHOOMP! WHOOMP!
THIS VOICE IN MY HEAD... LONTAR?
HELP!
HURRY!!
"IT'S ME INDEED, CLAIRE. THAT'S IT, GET INSIDE THAT HOLE, QUICK!!"
FUSHH!
ARG!
AHHH!
"SEE? THE DRAGON KNOWS YOU ARE THE ENEMY TO BE DEFEATED!
SWISHHH!

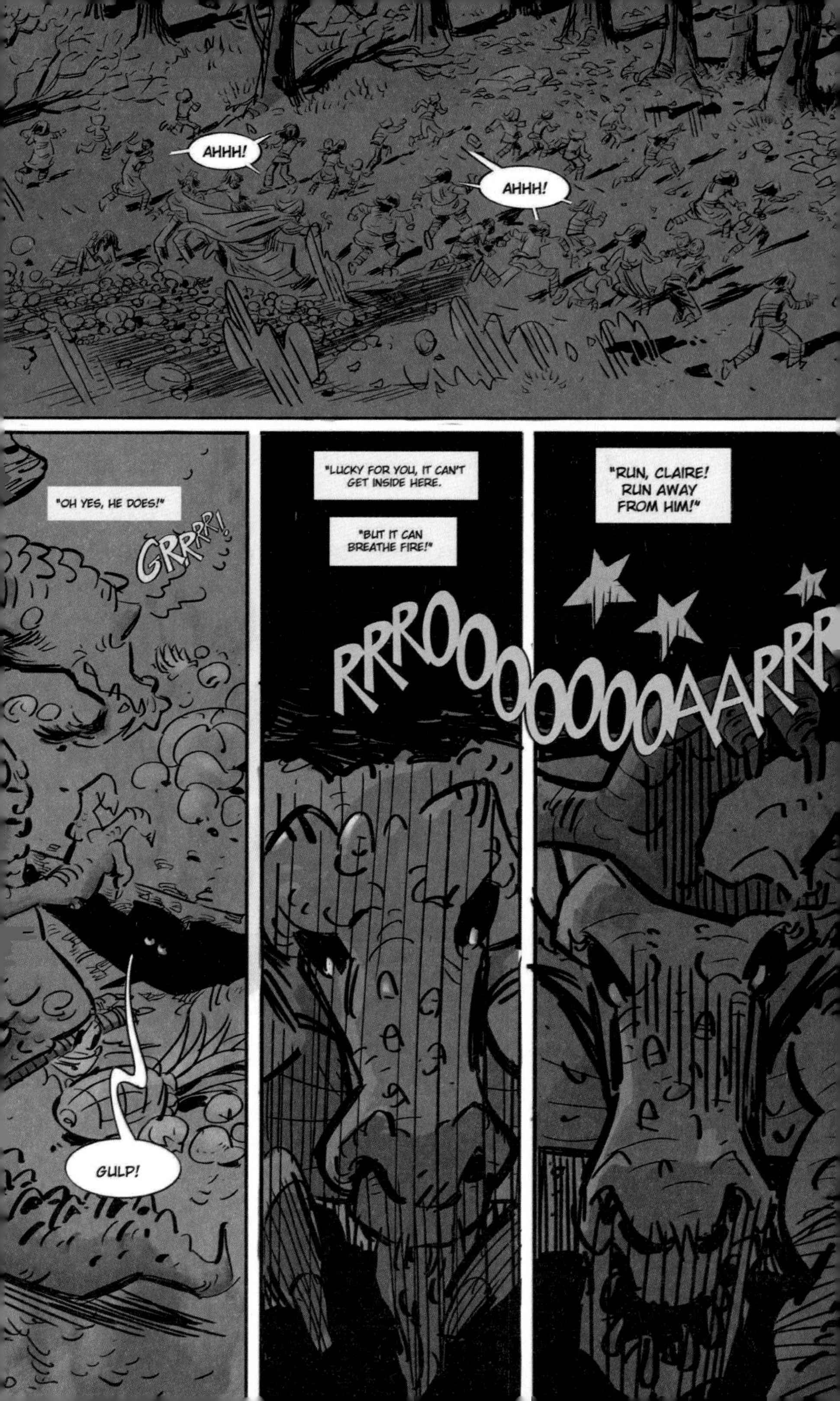
AHHH!
AHHH!
"OH YES, HE DOES!"
GRRRR!
GULP!
"LUCKY FOR YOU, IT CAN'T GET INSIDE HERE.
"BUT IT CAN BREATHE FIRE!"
"RUN, CLAIRE! RUN AWAY FROM HIM!"
RRROOOOOOOAARRR

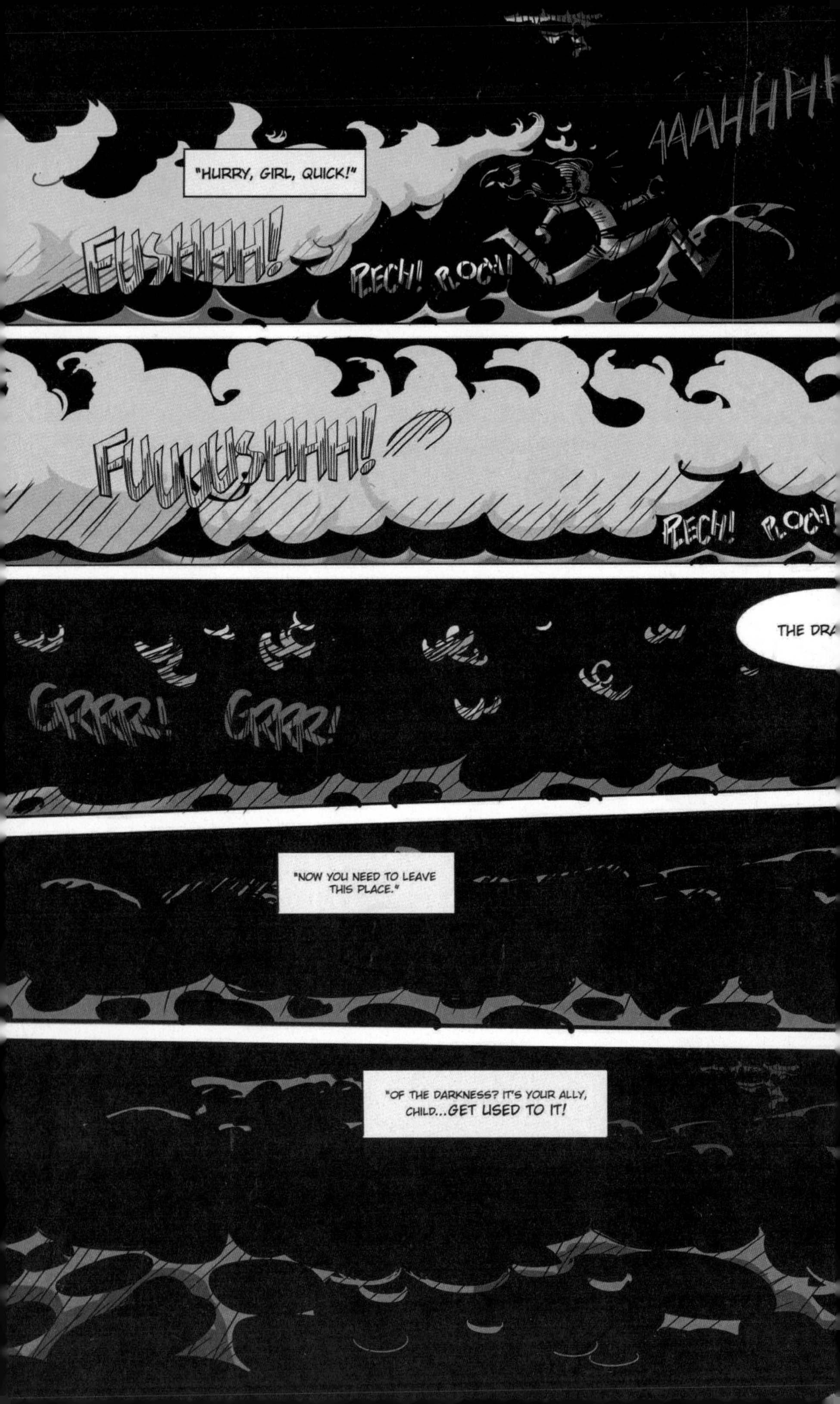
AAAHHHH
"HURRY, GIRL, QUICK!"
FUSHHH!
PLECH! PLOCH
FUUUSHHH!
PLECH! PLOCH
GRRR! GRRR!
THE DRA
"NOW YOU NEED TO LEAVE THIS PLACE."
"OF THE DARKNESS? IT'S YOUR ALLY, CHILD...GET USED TO IT!

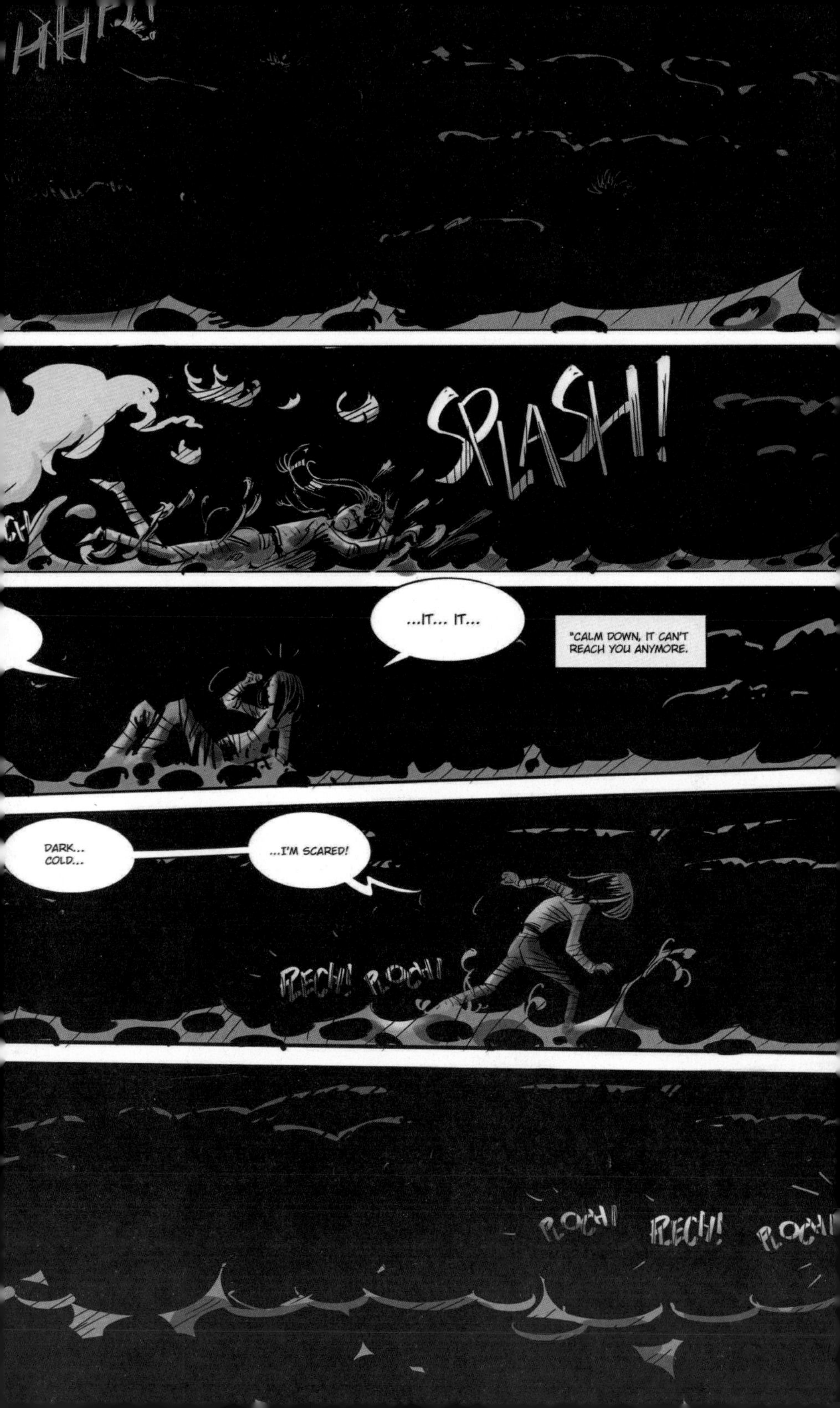

SPLASH!
...IT... IT...
"CALM DOWN, IT CAN'T REACH YOU ANYMORE.
DARK... COLD...
...I'M SCARED!
PLECH! PLOCH!
PLOCH! PLECH! PLOCH!

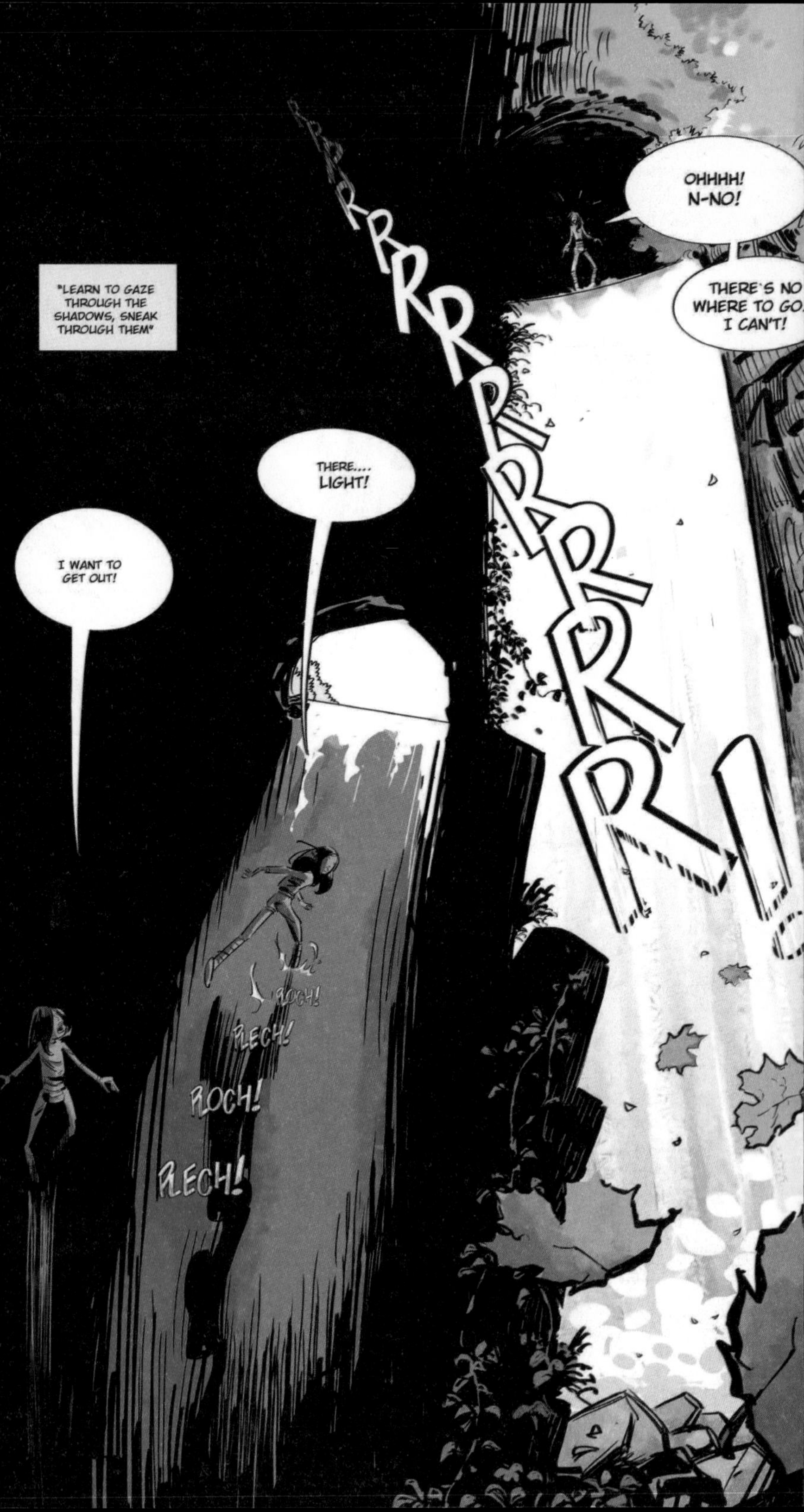
"LEARN TO GAZE THROUGH THE SHADOWS, SNEAK THROUGH THEM"
OHHHH! N-NO!
THERE'S NO WHERE TO GO. I CAN'T!
THERE.... LIGHT!
I WANT TO GET OUT!
PLOCH!
PLECH!
PLOCH!
PLECH!

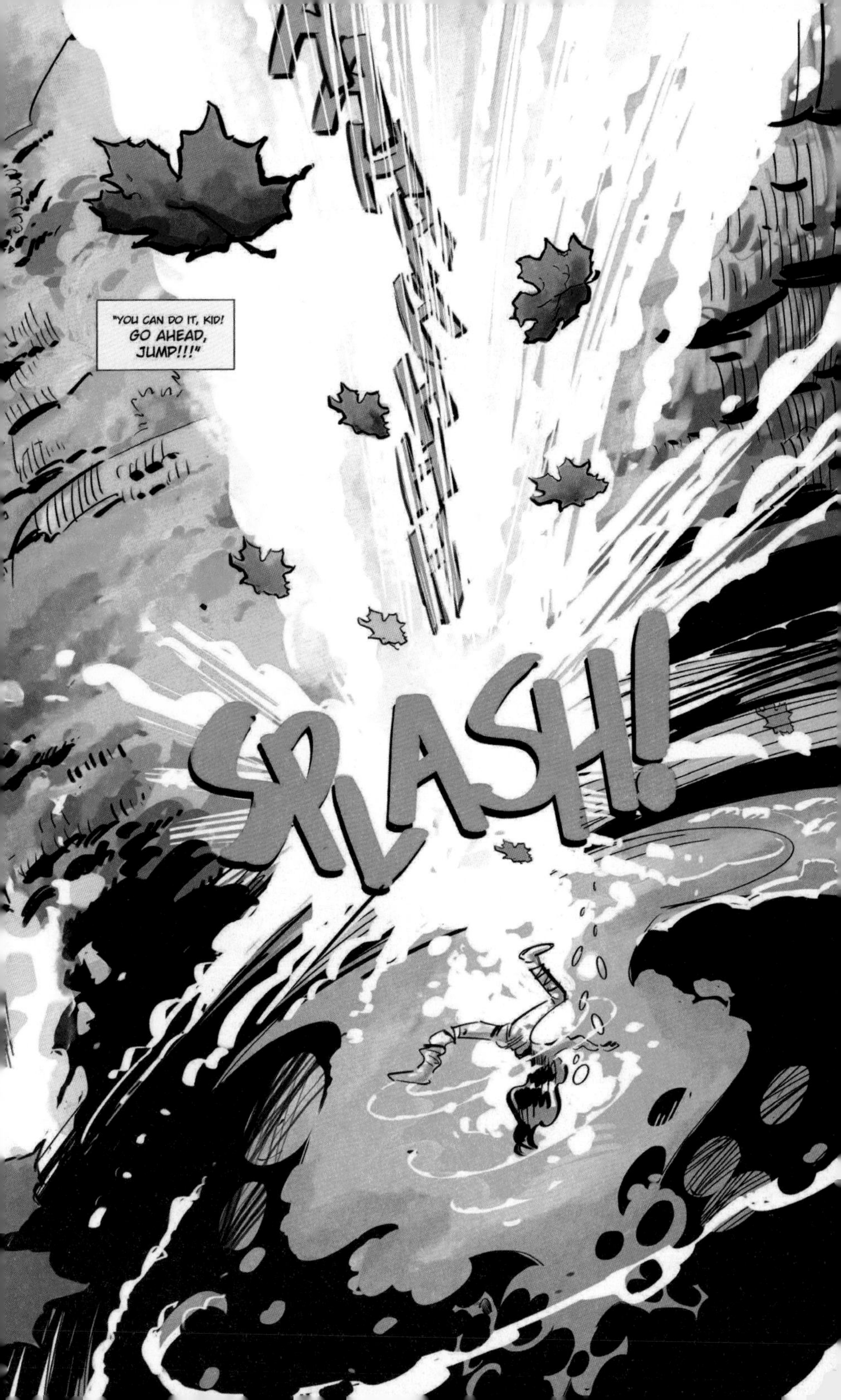
"YOU CAN DO IT, KID!
GO AHEAD,
JUMP!!!"
SPLASH!

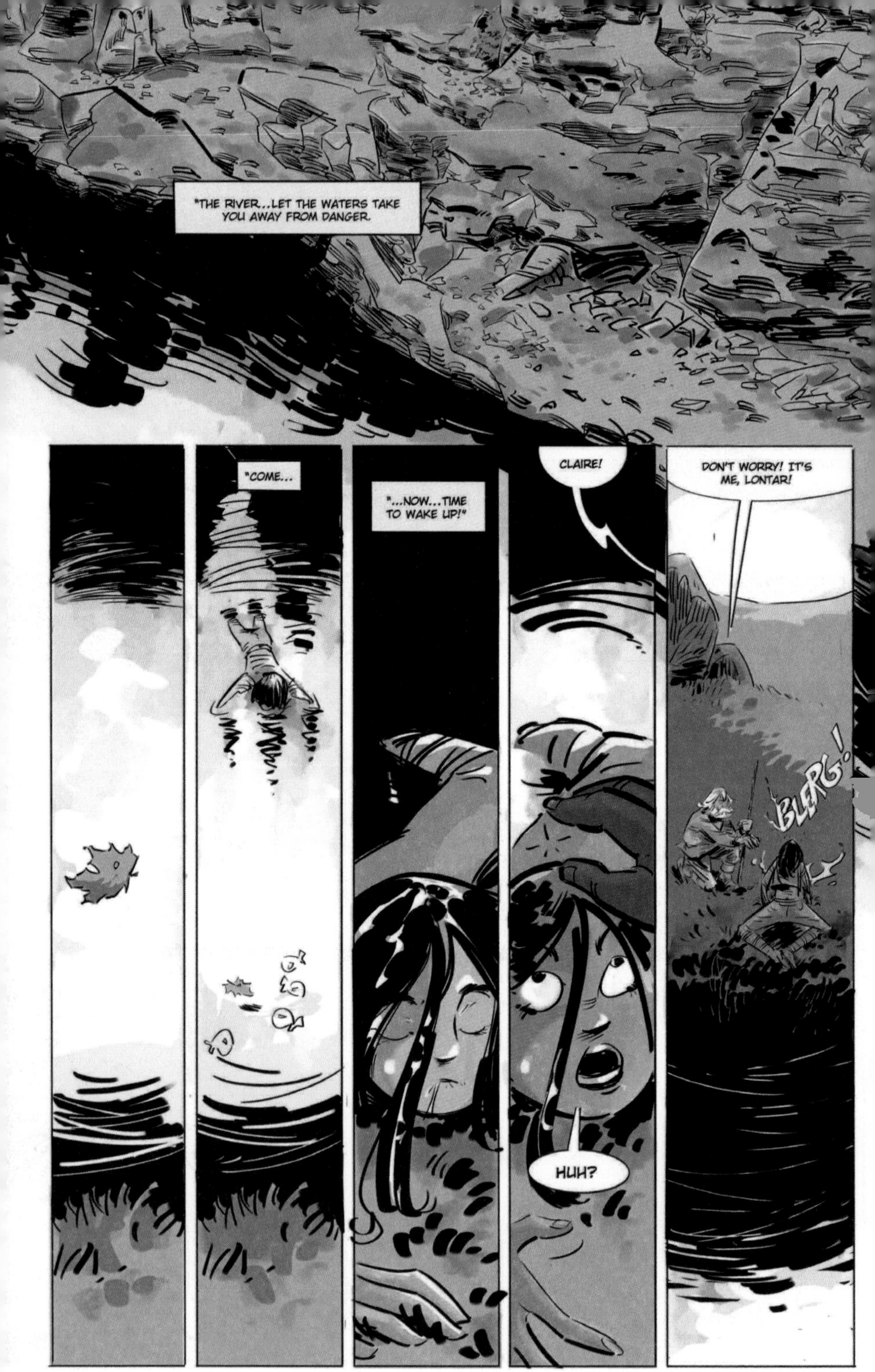
"THE RIVER...LET THE WATERS TAKE YOU AWAY FROM DANGER.
"COME...
"...NOW...TIME TO WAKE UP!"
CLAIRE!
HUH?
DON'T WORRY! IT'S ME, LONTAR!
BLERG!

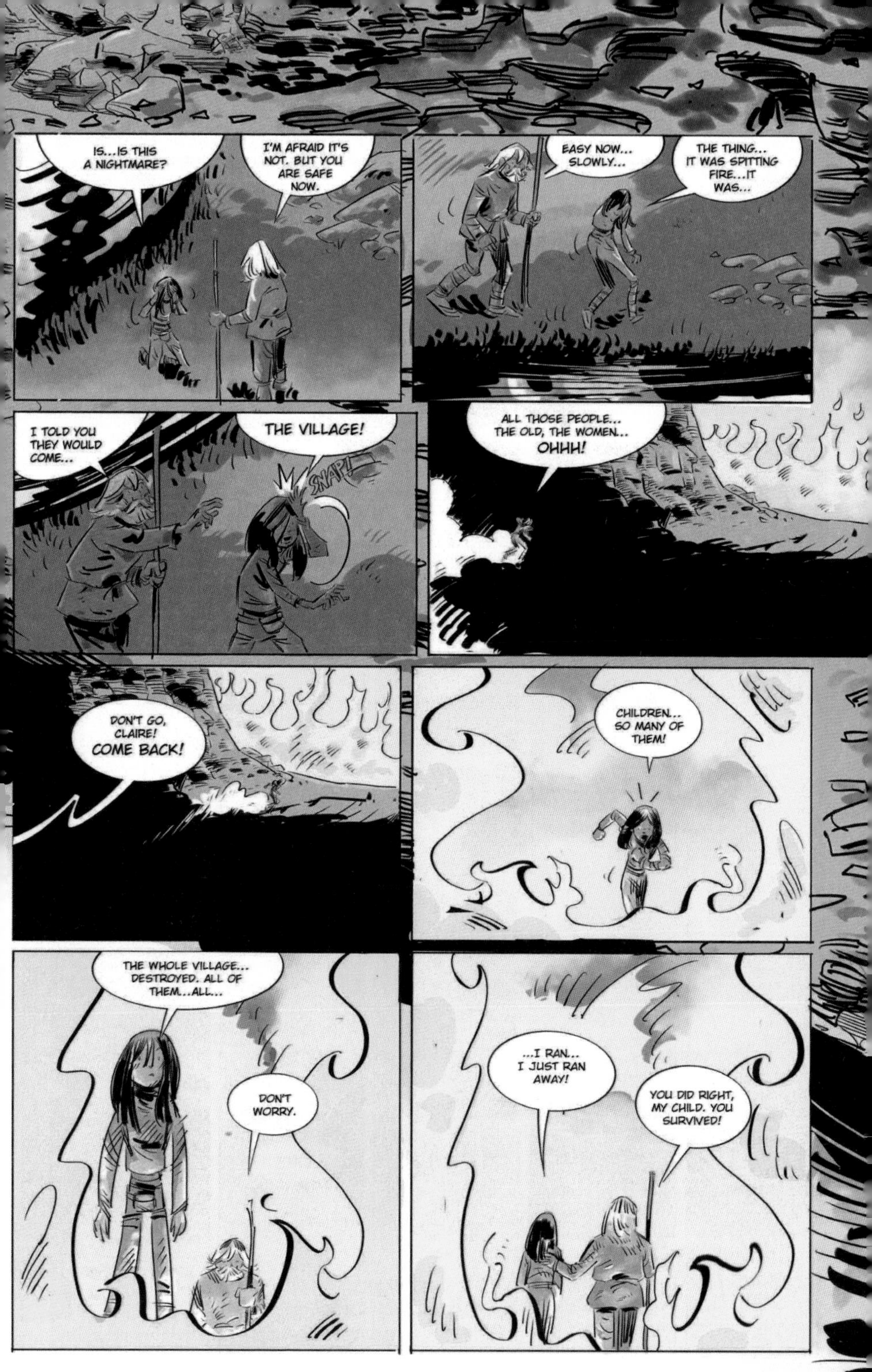
IS...IS THIS A NIGHTMARE?
I'M AFRAID IT'S NOT. BUT YOU ARE SAFE NOW.
EASY NOW... SLOWLY...
THE THING... IT WAS SPITTING FIRE...IT WAS...
I TOLD YOU THEY WOULD COME...
THE VILLAGE!
SNAP!
ALL THOSE PEOPLE... THE OLD, THE WOMEN... OHHH!
DON'T GO, CLAIRE! COME BACK!
CHILDREN... SO MANY OF THEM!
THE WHOLE VILLAGE... DESTROYED. ALL OF THEM...ALL...
DON'T WORRY.
...I RAN... I JUST RAN AWAY!
YOU DID RIGHT, MY CHILD. YOU SURVIVED!

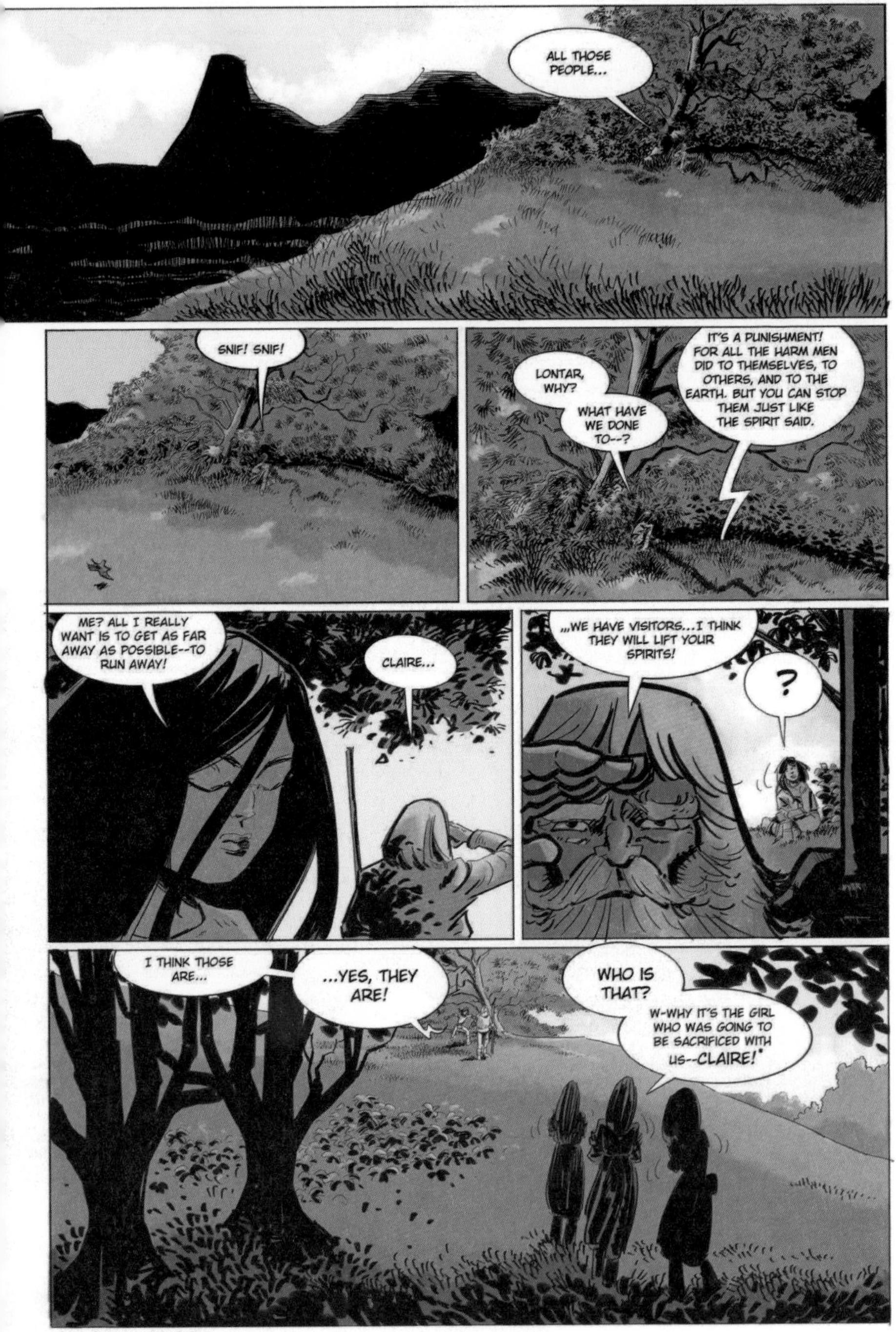
ALL THOSE PEOPLE...
SNIF! SNIF!
LONTAR, WHY?
WHAT HAVE WE DONE TO--?
IT'S A PUNISHMENT! FOR ALL THE HARM MEN DID TO THEMSELVES, TO OTHERS, AND TO THE EARTH. BUT YOU CAN STOP THEM JUST LIKE THE SPIRIT SAID.
ME? ALL I REALLY WANT IS TO GET AS FAR AWAY AS POSSIBLE--TO RUN AWAY!
CLAIRE...
...WE HAVE VISITORS...I THINK THEY WILL LIFT YOUR SPIRITS!
?
I THINK THOSE ARE...
...YES, THEY ARE!
WHO IS THAT?
W-WHY IT'S THE GIRL WHO WAS GOING TO BE SACRIFICED WITH US--CLAIRE!*

*SEE PREVIOUS EPISODE.

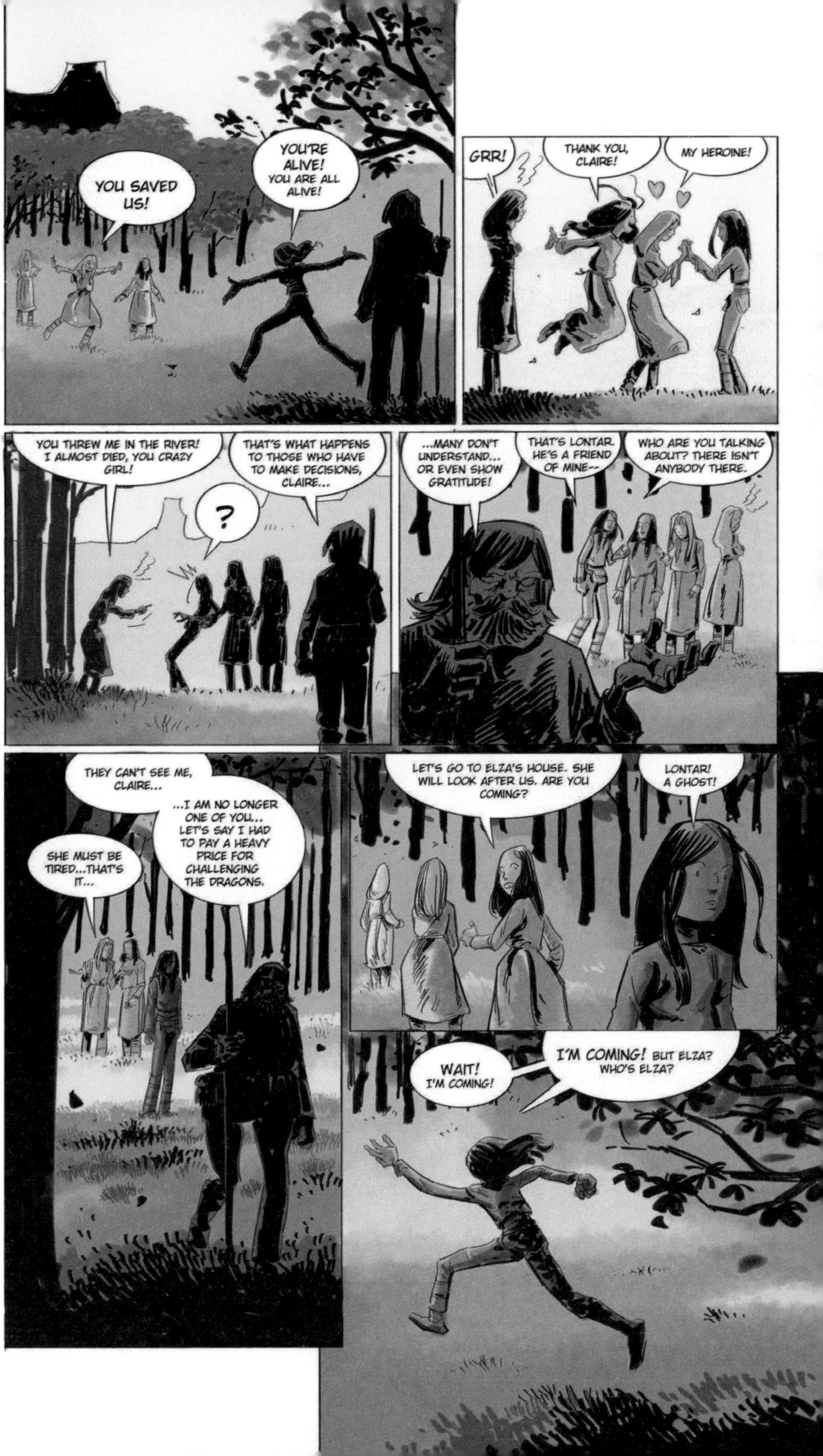
YOU SAVED US!
YOU'RE ALIVE! YOU ARE ALL ALIVE!
GRR!
THANK YOU, CLAIRE!
MY HEROINE!
YOU THREW ME IN THE RIVER! I ALMOST DIED, YOU CRAZY GIRL!
THAT'S WHAT HAPPENS TO THOSE WHO HAVE TO MAKE DECISIONS, CLAIRE...
?
...MANY DON'T UNDERSTAND... OR EVEN SHOW GRATITUDE!
THAT'S LONTAR. HE'S A FRIEND OF MINE--
WHO ARE YOU TALKING ABOUT? THERE ISN'T ANYBODY THERE.
THEY CAN'T SEE ME, CLAIRE...
...I AM NO LONGER ONE OF YOU... LET'S SAY I HAD TO PAY A HEAVY PRICE FOR CHALLENGING THE DRAGONS.
SHE MUST BE TIRED...THAT'S IT...
LET'S GO TO ELZA'S HOUSE. SHE WILL LOOK AFTER US. ARE YOU COMING?
LONTAR! A GHOST!
WAIT! I'M COMING!
I'M COMING! BUT ELZA? WHO'S ELZA?

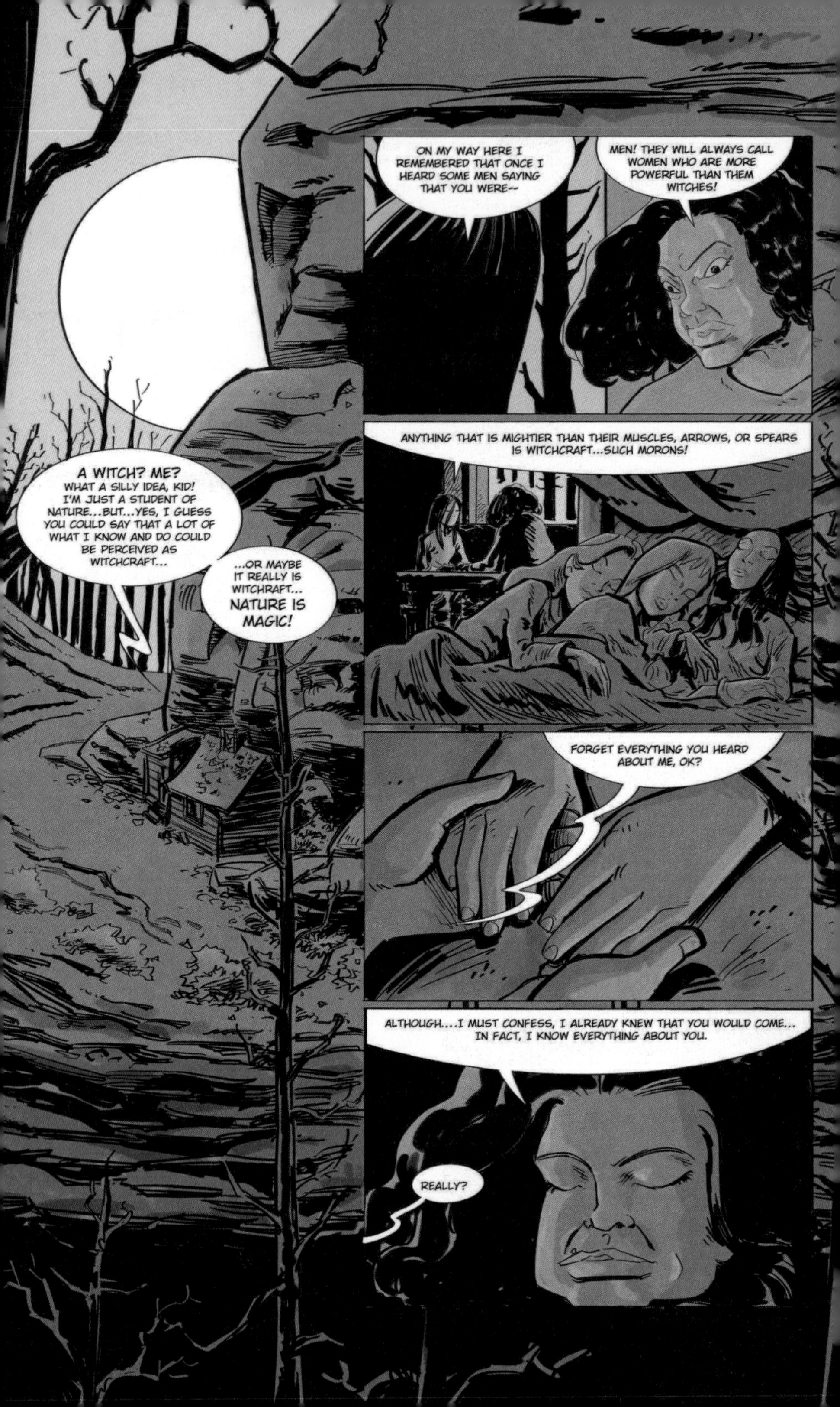
ON MY WAY HERE I REMEMBERED THAT ONCE I HEARD SOME MEN SAYING THAT YOU WERE--
MEN! THEY WILL ALWAYS CALL WOMEN WHO ARE MORE POWERFUL THAN THEM WITCHES!
A WITCH? ME? WHAT A SILLY IDEA, KID! I'M JUST A STUDENT OF NATURE...BUT...YES, I GUESS YOU COULD SAY THAT A LOT OF WHAT I KNOW AND DO COULD BE PERCEIVED AS WITCHCRAFT...
...OR MAYBE IT REALLY IS WITCHCRAFT... NATURE IS MAGIC!
ANYTHING THAT IS MIGHTIER THAN THEIR MUSCLES, ARROWS, OR SPEARS IS WITCHCRAFT...SUCH MORONS!
FORGET EVERYTHING YOU HEARD ABOUT ME, OK?
ALTHOUGH....I MUST CONFESS, I ALREADY KNEW THAT YOU WOULD COME... IN FACT, I KNOW EVERYTHING ABOUT YOU.
REALLY?

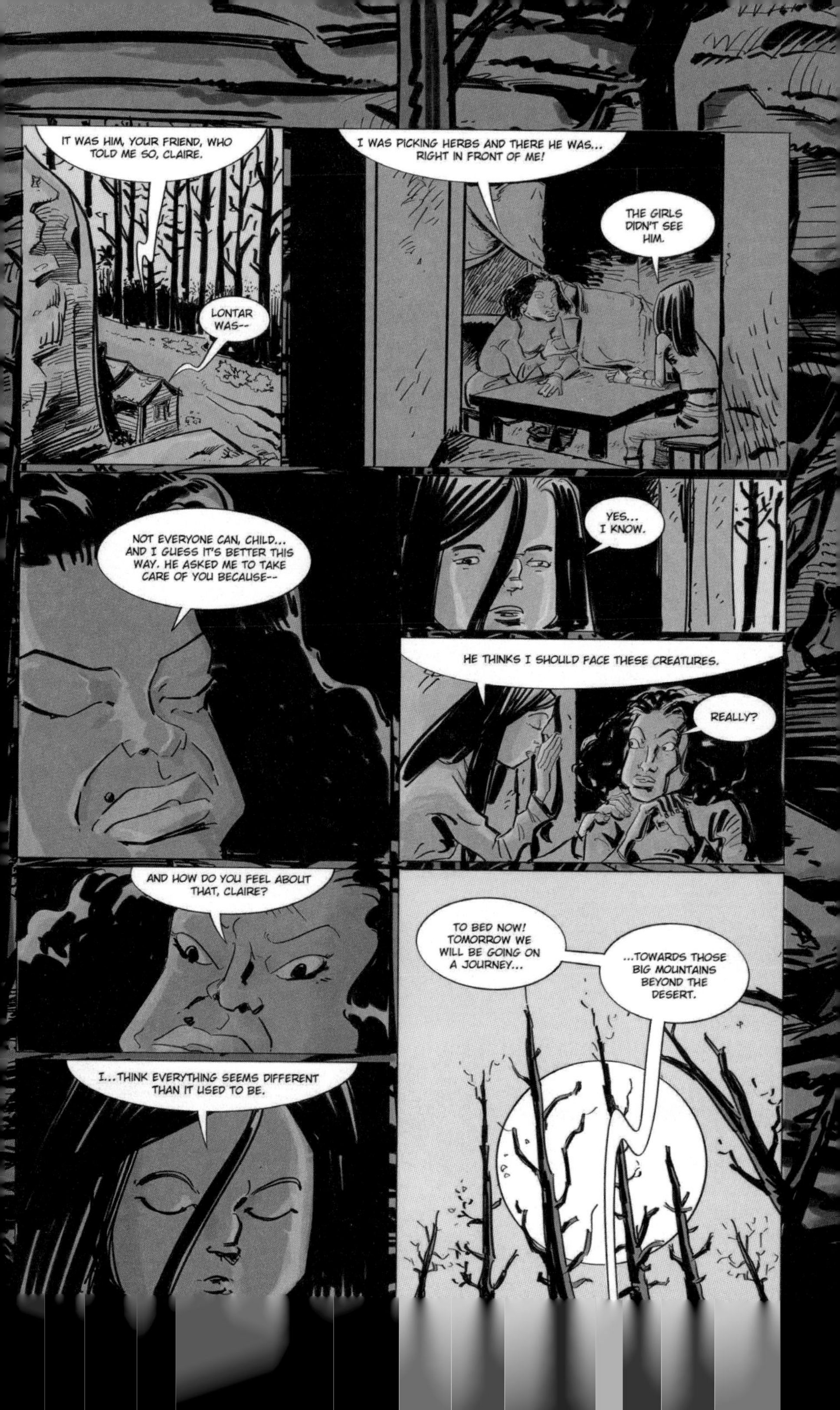

IT WAS HIM, YOUR FRIEND, WHO TOLD ME SO, CLAIRE.
LONTAR WAS--
I WAS PICKING HERBS AND THERE HE WAS... RIGHT IN FRONT OF ME!
THE GIRLS DIDN'T SEE HIM.
NOT EVERYONE CAN, CHILD... AND I GUESS IT'S BETTER THIS WAY. HE ASKED ME TO TAKE CARE OF YOU BECAUSE--
YES... I KNOW.
HE THINKS I SHOULD FACE THESE CREATURES.
REALLY?
AND HOW DO YOU FEEL ABOUT THAT, CLAIRE?
I...THINK EVERYTHING SEEMS DIFFERENT THAN IT USED TO BE.
TO BED NOW! TOMORROW WE WILL BE GOING ON A JOURNEY...
...TOWARDS THOSE BIG MOUNTAINS BEYOND THE DESERT.

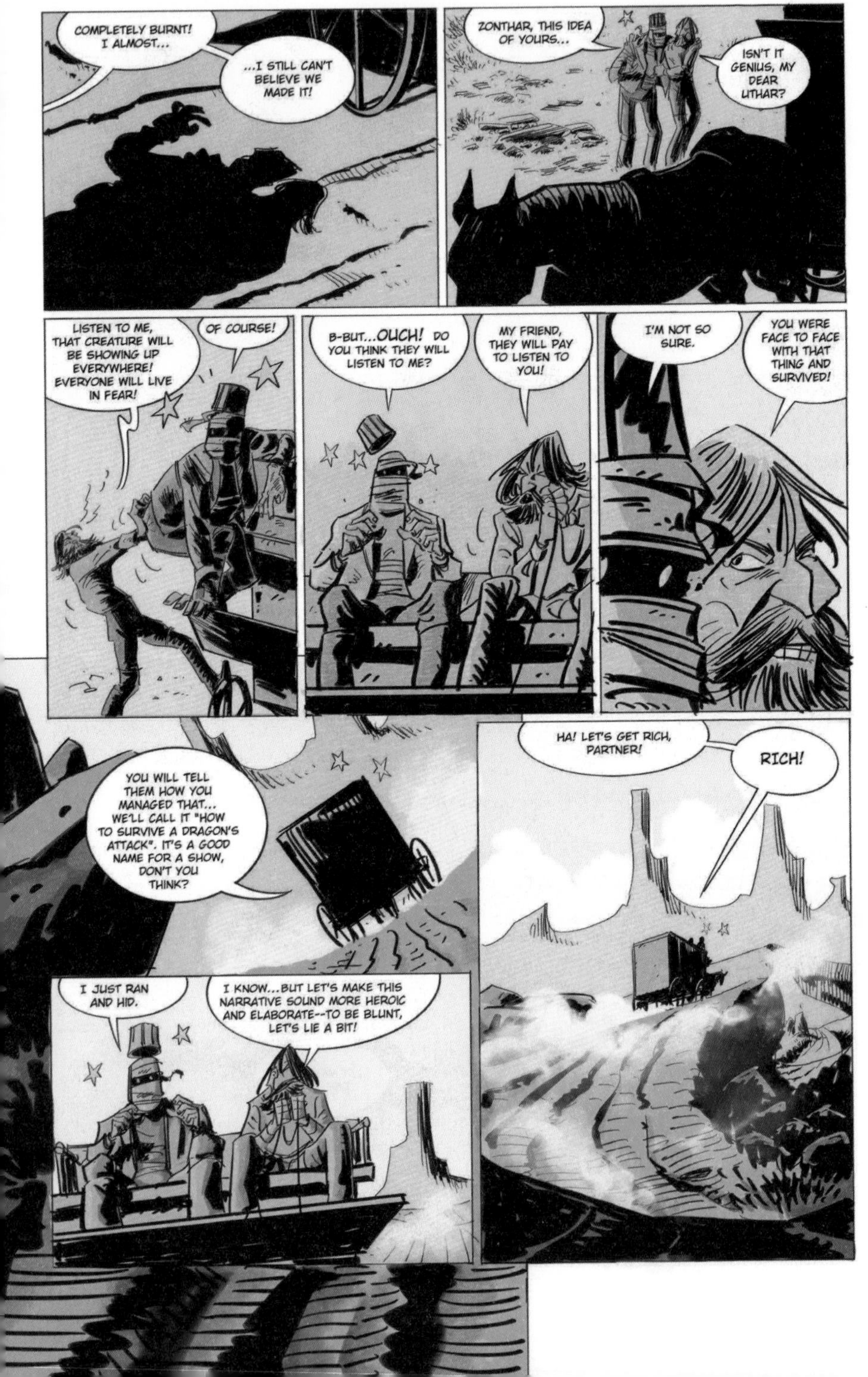
COMPLETELY BURNT! I ALMOST...
...I STILL CAN'T BELIEVE WE MADE IT!
ZONTHAR, THIS IDEA OF YOURS...
ISN'T IT GENIUS, MY DEAR UTHAR?
LISTEN TO ME, THAT CREATURE WILL BE SHOWING UP EVERYWHERE! EVERYONE WILL LIVE IN FEAR!
OF COURSE!
B-BUT...OUCH! DO YOU THINK THEY WILL LISTEN TO ME?
MY FRIEND, THEY WILL PAY TO LISTEN TO YOU!
I'M NOT SO SURE.
YOU WERE FACE TO FACE WITH THAT THING AND SURVIVED!
YOU WILL TELL THEM HOW YOU MANAGED THAT... WE'LL CALL IT "HOW TO SURVIVE A DRAGON'S ATTACK". IT'S A GOOD NAME FOR A SHOW, DON'T YOU THINK?
I JUST RAN AND HID.
I KNOW...BUT LET'S MAKE THIS NARRATIVE SOUND MORE HEROIC AND ELABORATE--TO BE BLUNT, LET'S LIE A BIT!
HA! LET'S GET RICH, PARTNER!
RICH!

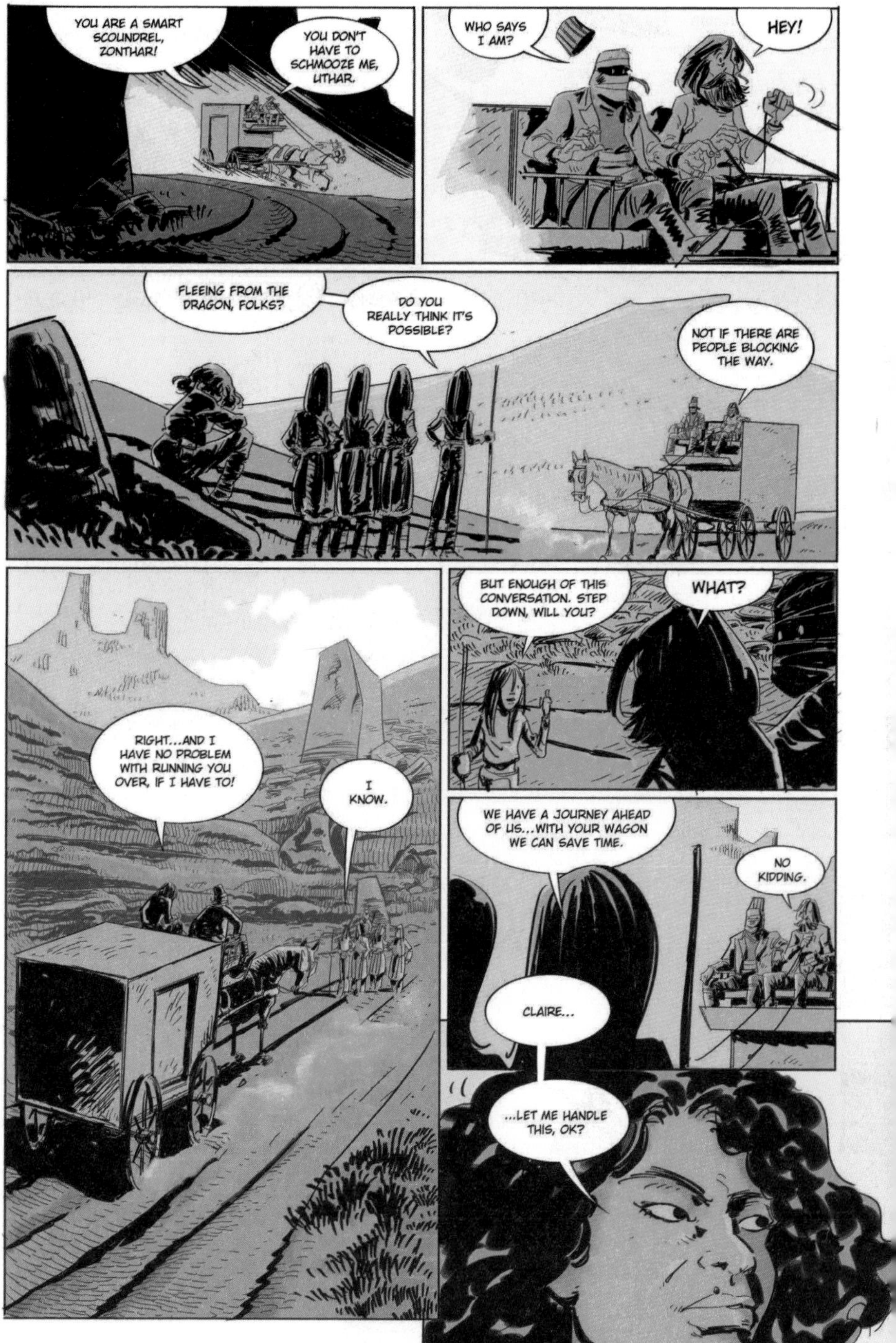

YOU ARE A SMART SCOUNDREL, ZONTHAR!
YOU DON'T HAVE TO SCHMOOZE ME, UTHAR.
WHO SAYS I AM?
HEY!
FLEEING FROM THE DRAGON, FOLKS?
DO YOU REALLY THINK IT'S POSSIBLE?
NOT IF THERE ARE PEOPLE BLOCKING THE WAY.
RIGHT...AND I HAVE NO PROBLEM WITH RUNNING YOU OVER, IF I HAVE TO!
I KNOW.
BUT ENOUGH OF THIS CONVERSATION. STEP DOWN, WILL YOU?
WHAT?
WE HAVE A JOURNEY AHEAD OF US...WITH YOUR WAGON WE CAN SAVE TIME.
NO KIDDING.
CLAIRE...
...LET ME HANDLE THIS, OK?

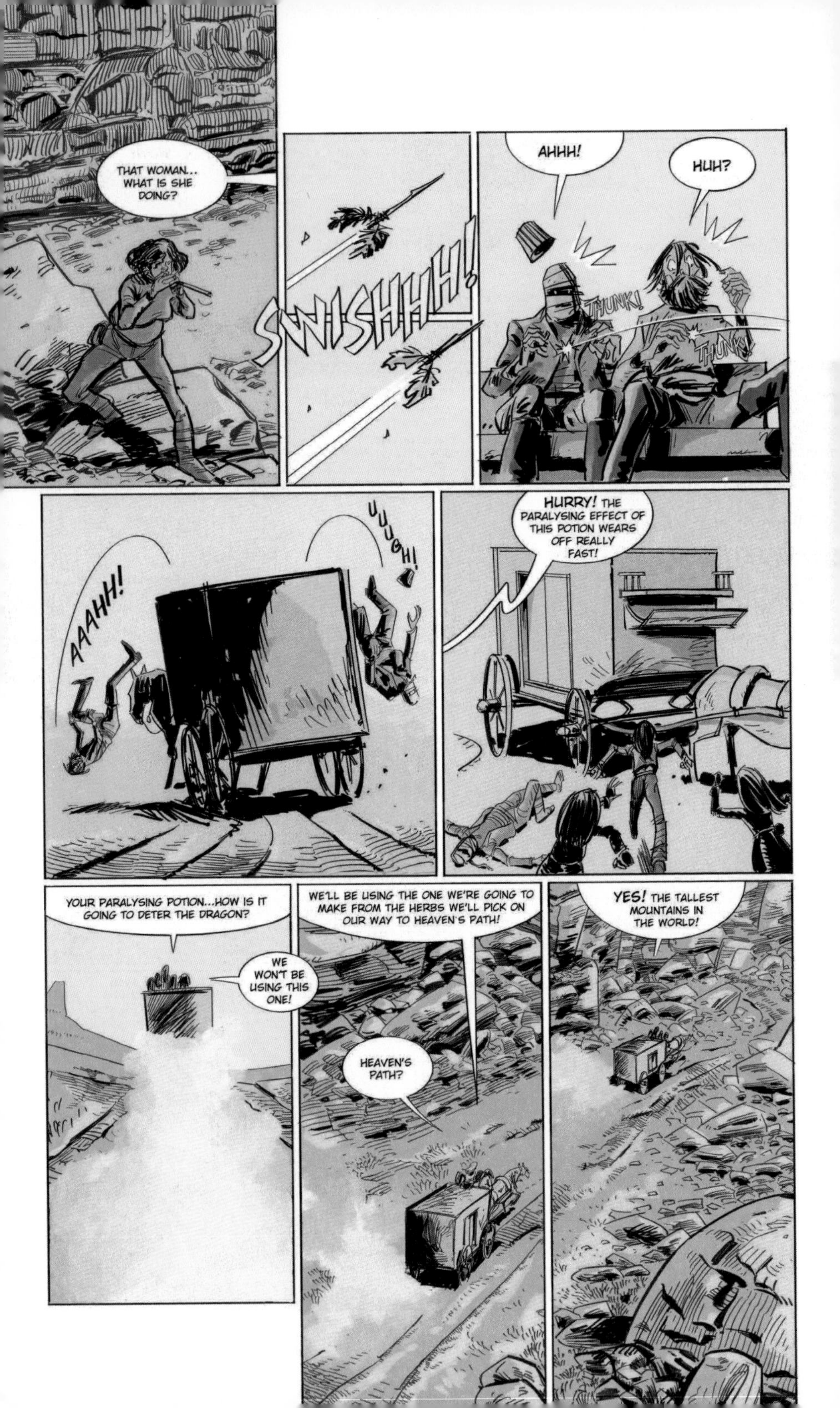

THAT WOMAN... WHAT IS SHE DOING?
SWISHHH!
AHHH!
HUH?
THUNK!
THUNK!
AAAHH!
UUUGH!
HURRY! THE PARALYSING EFFECT OF THIS POTION WEARS OFF REALLY FAST!
YOUR PARALYSING POTION...HOW IS IT GOING TO DETER THE DRAGON?
WE WON'T BE USING THIS ONE!
WE'LL BE USING THE ONE WE'RE GOING TO MAKE FROM THE HERBS WE'LL PICK ON OUR WAY TO HEAVEN'S PATH!
HEAVEN'S PATH?
YES! THE TALLEST MOUNTAINS IN THE WORLD!

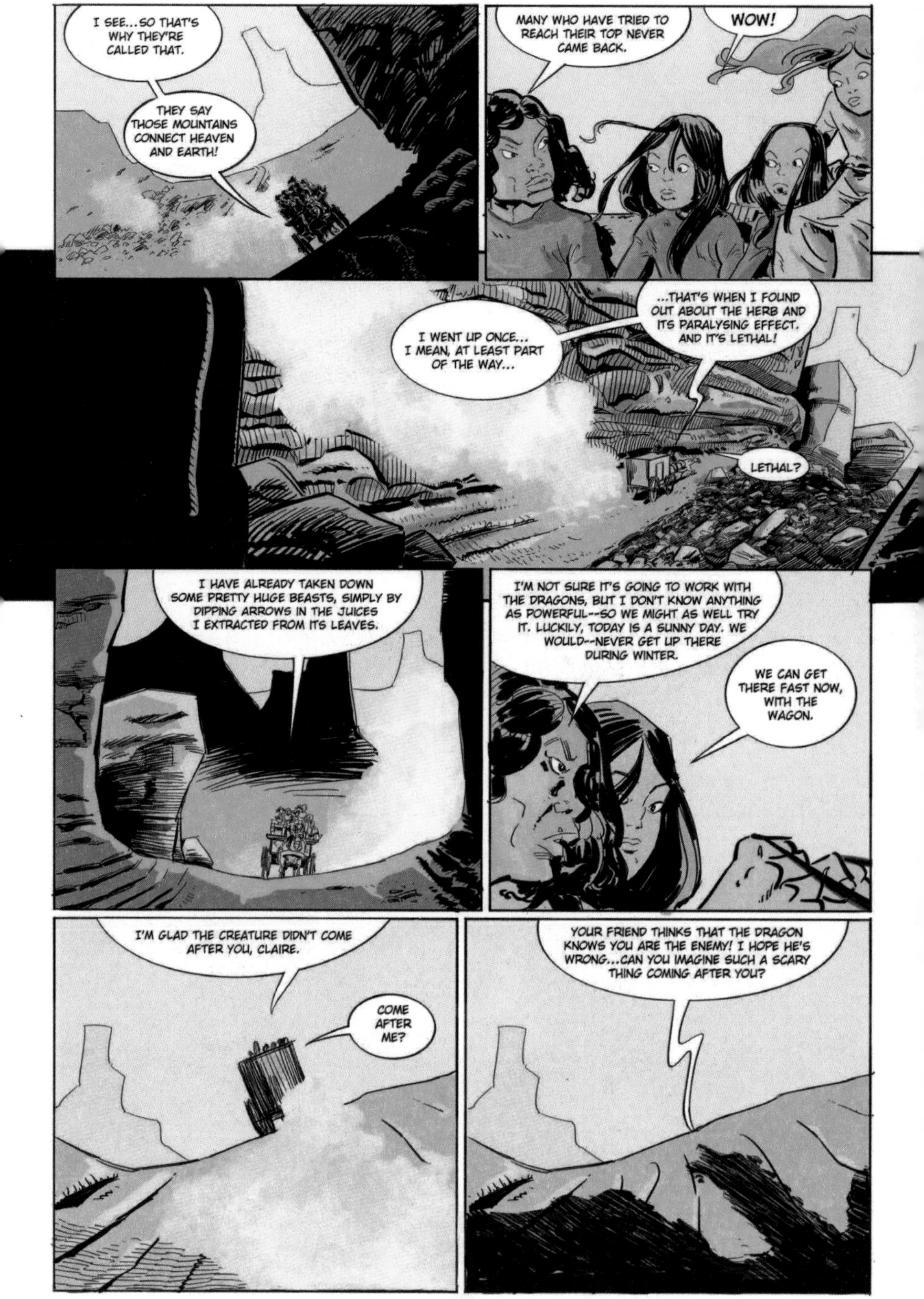
I SEE...SO THAT'S WHY THEY'RE CALLED THAT.
THEY SAY THOSE MOUNTAINS CONNECT HEAVEN AND EARTH!
MANY WHO HAVE TRIED TO REACH THEIR TOP NEVER CAME BACK.
WOW!
I WENT UP ONCE... I MEAN, AT LEAST PART OF THE WAY...
...THAT'S WHEN I FOUND OUT ABOUT THE HERB AND ITS PARALYSING EFFECT. AND IT'S LETHAL!
LETHAL?
I HAVE ALREADY TAKEN DOWN SOME PRETTY HUGE BEASTS, SIMPLY BY DIPPING ARROWS IN THE JUICES I EXTRACTED FROM ITS LEAVES.
I'M NOT SURE IT'S GOING TO WORK WITH THE DRAGONS, BUT I DON'T KNOW ANYTHING AS POWERFUL--SO WE MIGHT AS WELL TRY IT. LUCKILY, TODAY IS A SUNNY DAY. WE WOULD--NEVER GET UP THERE DURING WINTER.
WE CAN GET THERE FAST NOW, WITH THE WAGON.
I'M GLAD THE CREATURE DIDN'T COME AFTER YOU, CLAIRE.
COME AFTER ME?
YOUR FRIEND THINKS THAT THE DRAGON KNOWS YOU ARE THE ENEMY! I HOPE HE'S WRONG...CAN YOU IMAGINE SUCH A SCARY THING COMING AFTER YOU?

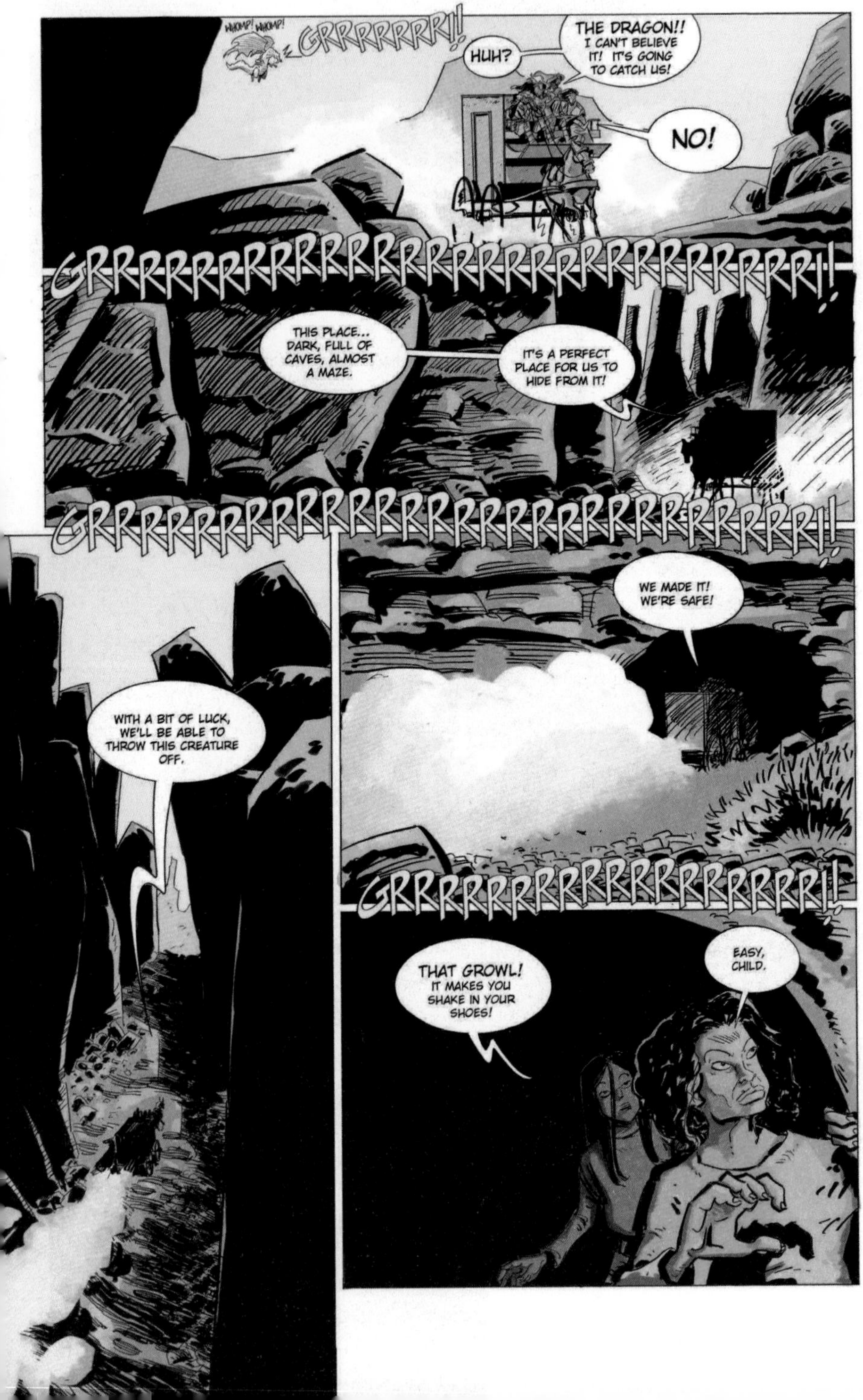

WHOMP! WHOMP!
GRRRRRRR!!
HUH?
THE DRAGON!! I CAN'T BELIEVE IT! IT'S GOING TO CATCH US!
NO!
GRRRRRRRRRRRRRRRRRRRRRRRRRRRRR!!
THIS PLACE... DARK, FULL OF CAVES, ALMOST A MAZE.
IT'S A PERFECT PLACE FOR US TO HIDE FROM IT!
GRRRRRRRRRRRRRRRRRRRRRRRRRRRRR!!
WITH A BIT OF LUCK, WE'LL BE ABLE TO THROW THIS CREATURE OFF.
WE MADE IT! WE'RE SAFE!
GRRRRRRRRRRRRRRRRRRRR!!
THAT GROWL! IT MAKES YOU SHAKE IN YOUR SHOES!
EASY, CHILD.

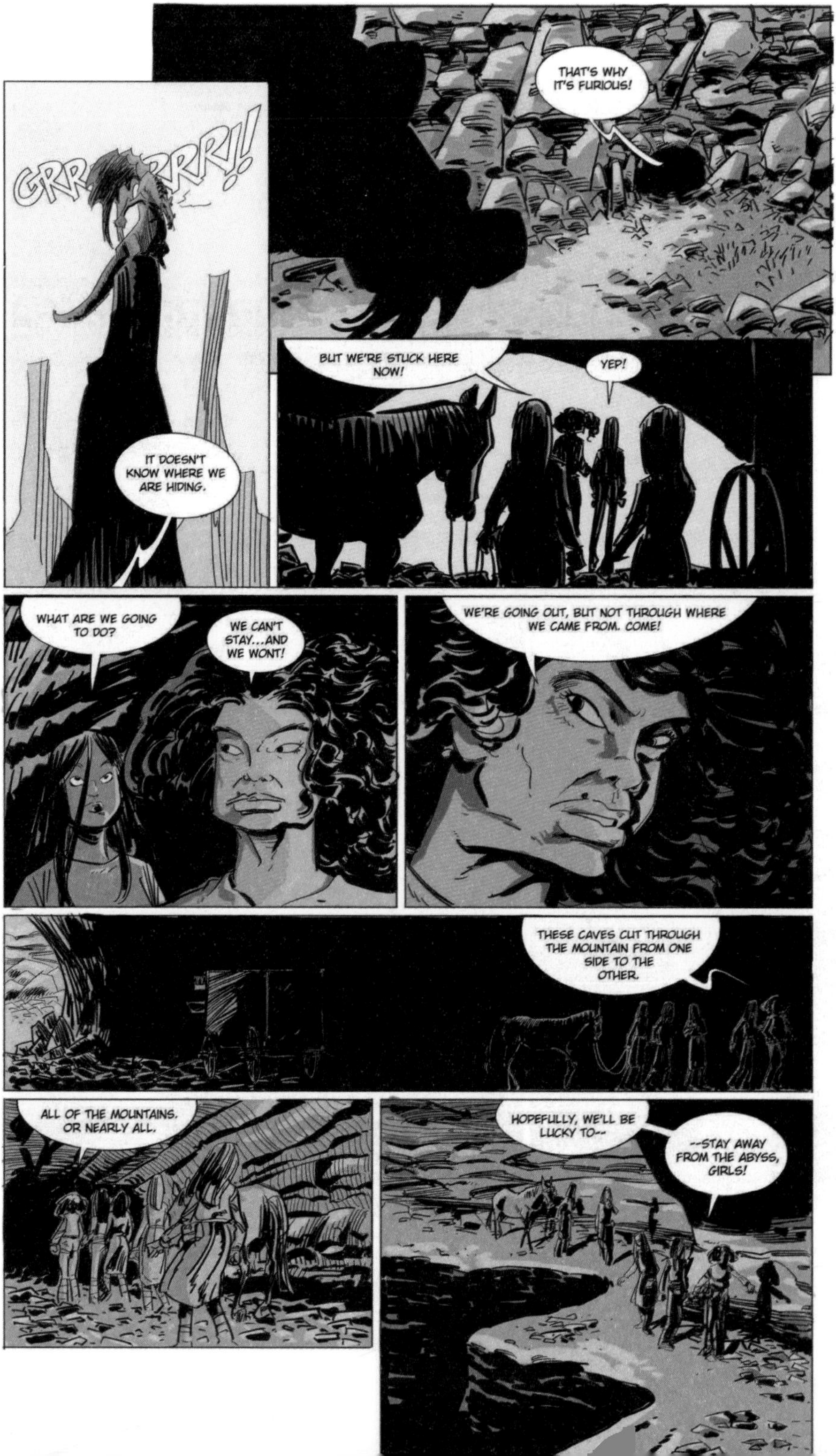
GRRRRRR!!
THAT'S WHY IT'S FURIOUS!
IT DOESN'T KNOW WHERE WE ARE HIDING.
BUT WE'RE STUCK HERE NOW!
YEP!
WHAT ARE WE GOING TO DO?
WE CAN'T STAY...AND WE WONT!
WE'RE GOING OUT, BUT NOT THROUGH WHERE WE CAME FROM. COME!
THESE CAVES CUT THROUGH THE MOUNTAIN FROM ONE SIDE TO THE OTHER.
ALL OF THE MOUNTAINS. OR NEARLY ALL.
HOPEFULLY, WE'LL BE LUCKY TO--
--STAY AWAY FROM THE ABYSS, GIRLS!

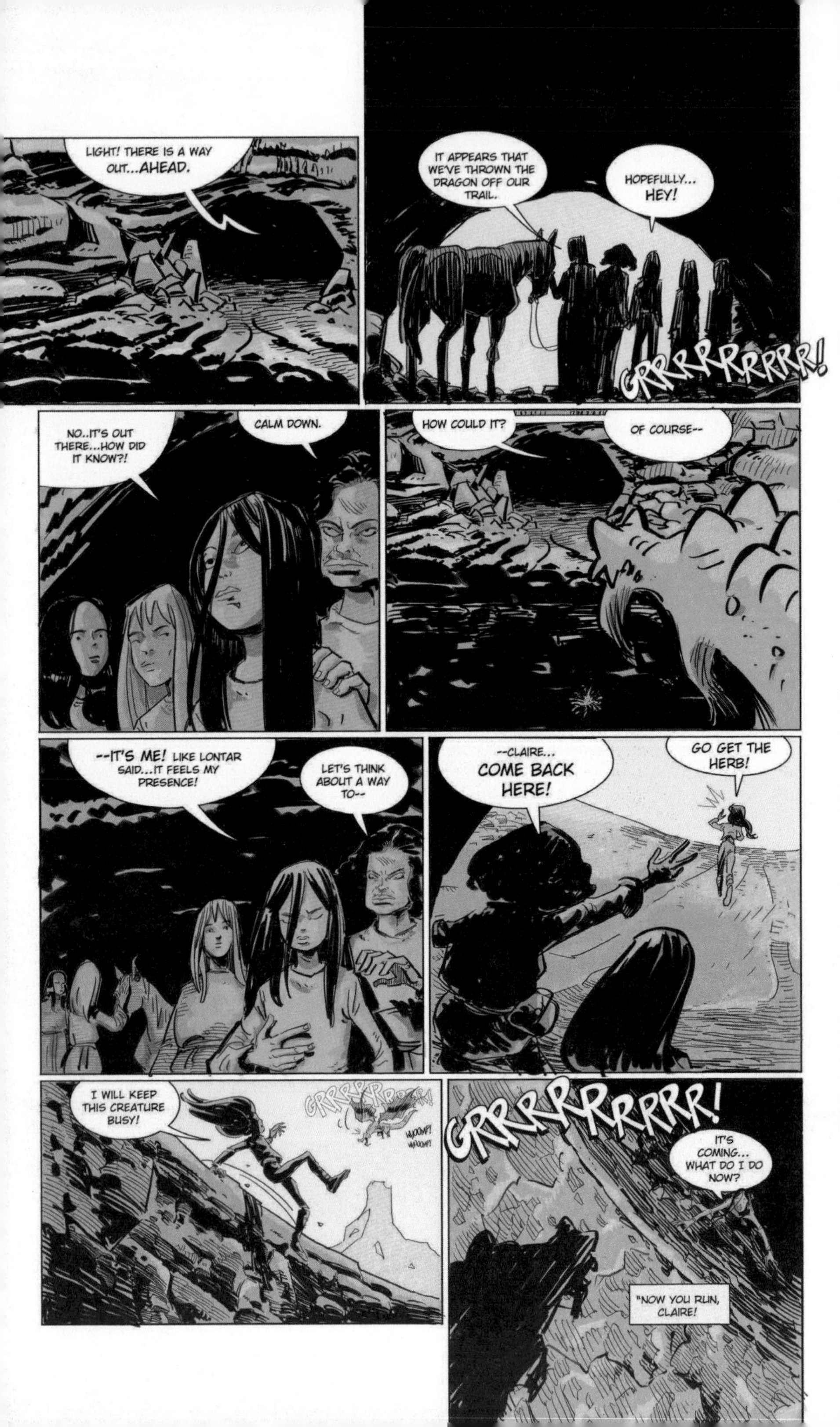
LIGHT! THERE IS A WAY OUT...AHEAD.
IT APPEARS THAT WE'VE THROWN THE DRAGON OFF OUR TRAIL.
HOPEFULLY... HEY!
GRRRRRRRRR!
NO..IT'S OUT THERE...HOW DID IT KNOW?!
CALM DOWN.
HOW COULD IT?
OF COURSE--
--IT'S ME! LIKE LONTAR SAID...IT FEELS MY PRESENCE!
LET'S THINK ABOUT A WAY TO--
--CLAIRE... COME BACK HERE!
GO GET THE HERB!
I WILL KEEP THIS CREATURE BUSY!
WHOOMP! WHOOMP!
GRRRRRRRRR!
IT'S COMING... WHAT DO I DO NOW?
"NOW YOU RUN, CLAIRE!

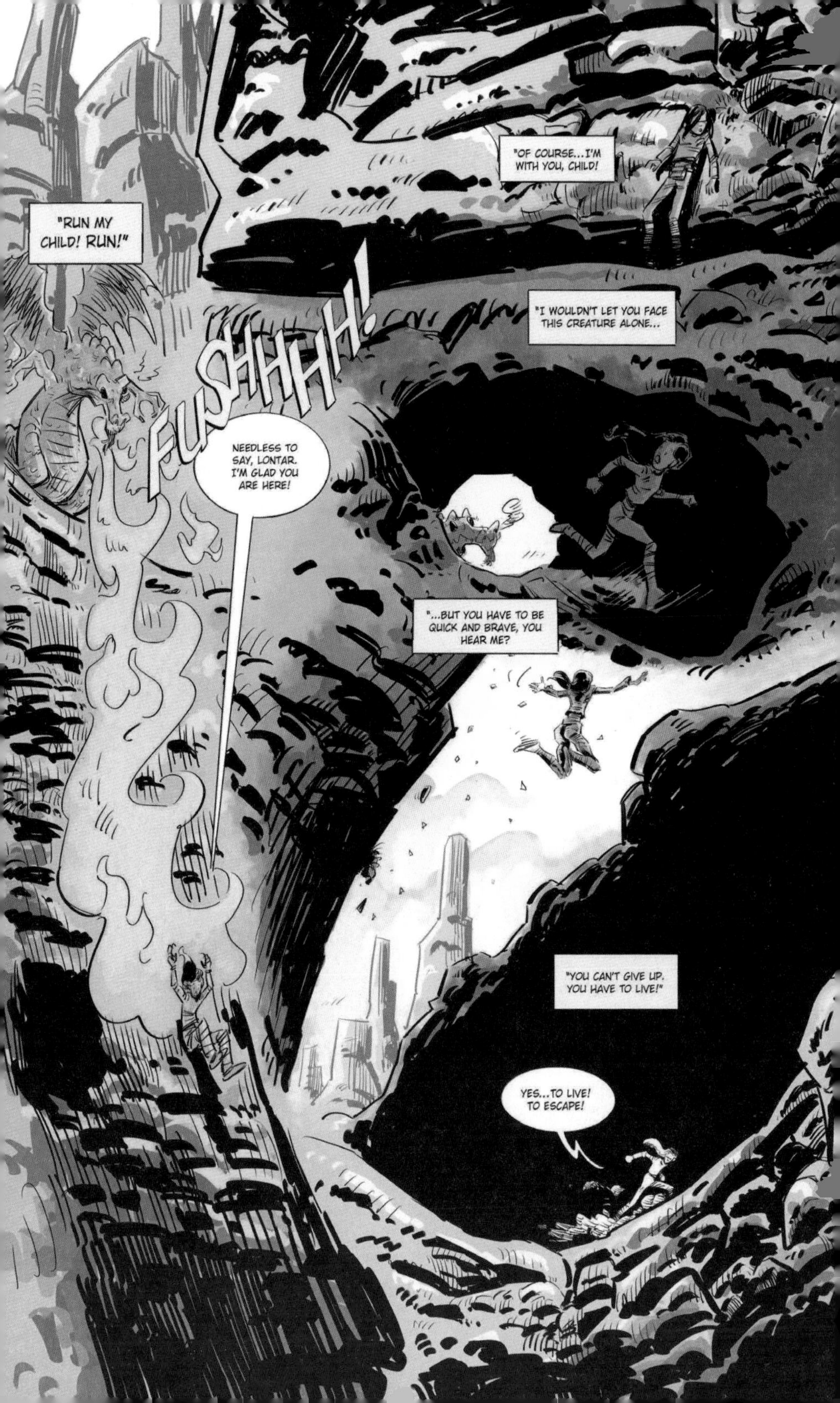
"OF COURSE...I'M WITH YOU, CHILD!
"RUN MY CHILD! RUN!"
"I WOULDN'T LET YOU FACE THIS CREATURE ALONE...
FUSHHHH!
NEEDLESS TO SAY, LONTAR. I'M GLAD YOU ARE HERE!
"...BUT YOU HAVE TO BE QUICK AND BRAVE, YOU HEAR ME?
"YOU CAN'T GIVE UP. YOU HAVE TO LIVE!"
YES...TO LIVE! TO ESCAPE!

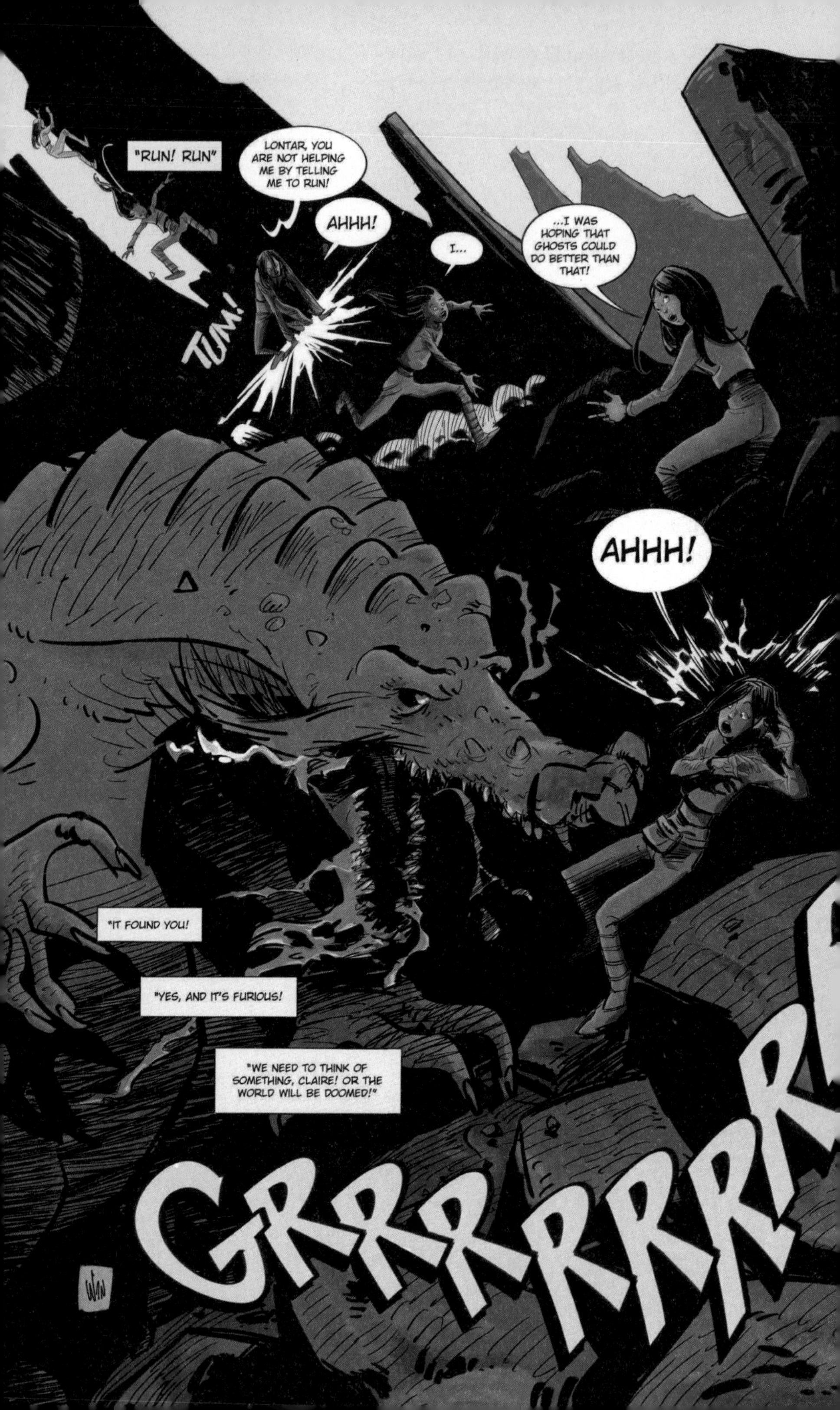
"RUN! RUN"
LONTAR, YOU ARE NOT HELPING ME BY TELLING ME TO RUN!
AHHH!
TUM!
I...
...I WAS HOPING THAT GHOSTS COULD DO BETTER THAN THAT!
AHHH!
"IT FOUND YOU!
"YES, AND IT'S FURIOUS!
"WE NEED TO THINK OF SOMETHING, CLAIRE! OR THE WORLD WILL BE DOOMED!"
GRRRRRRR

CHAPTER 3

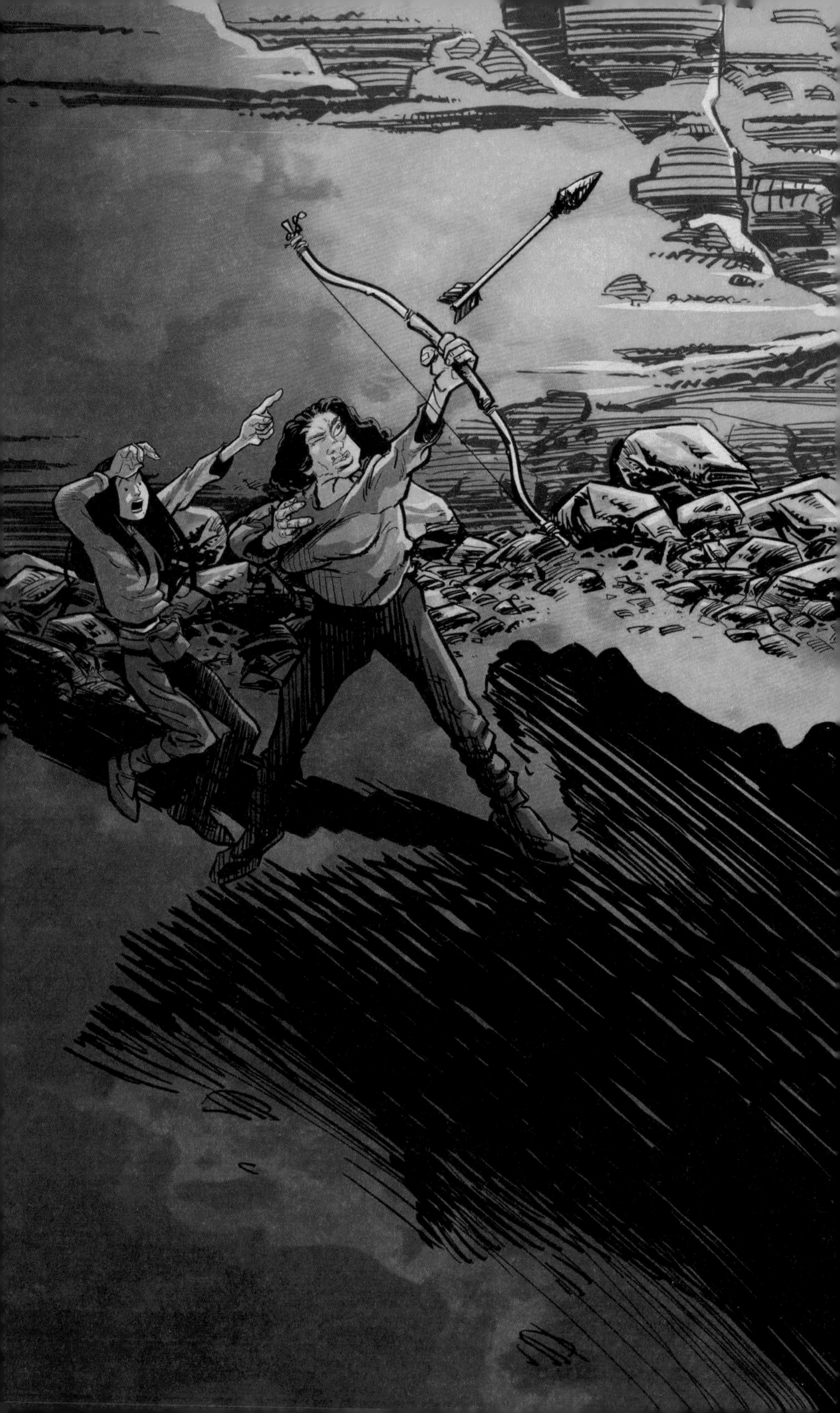

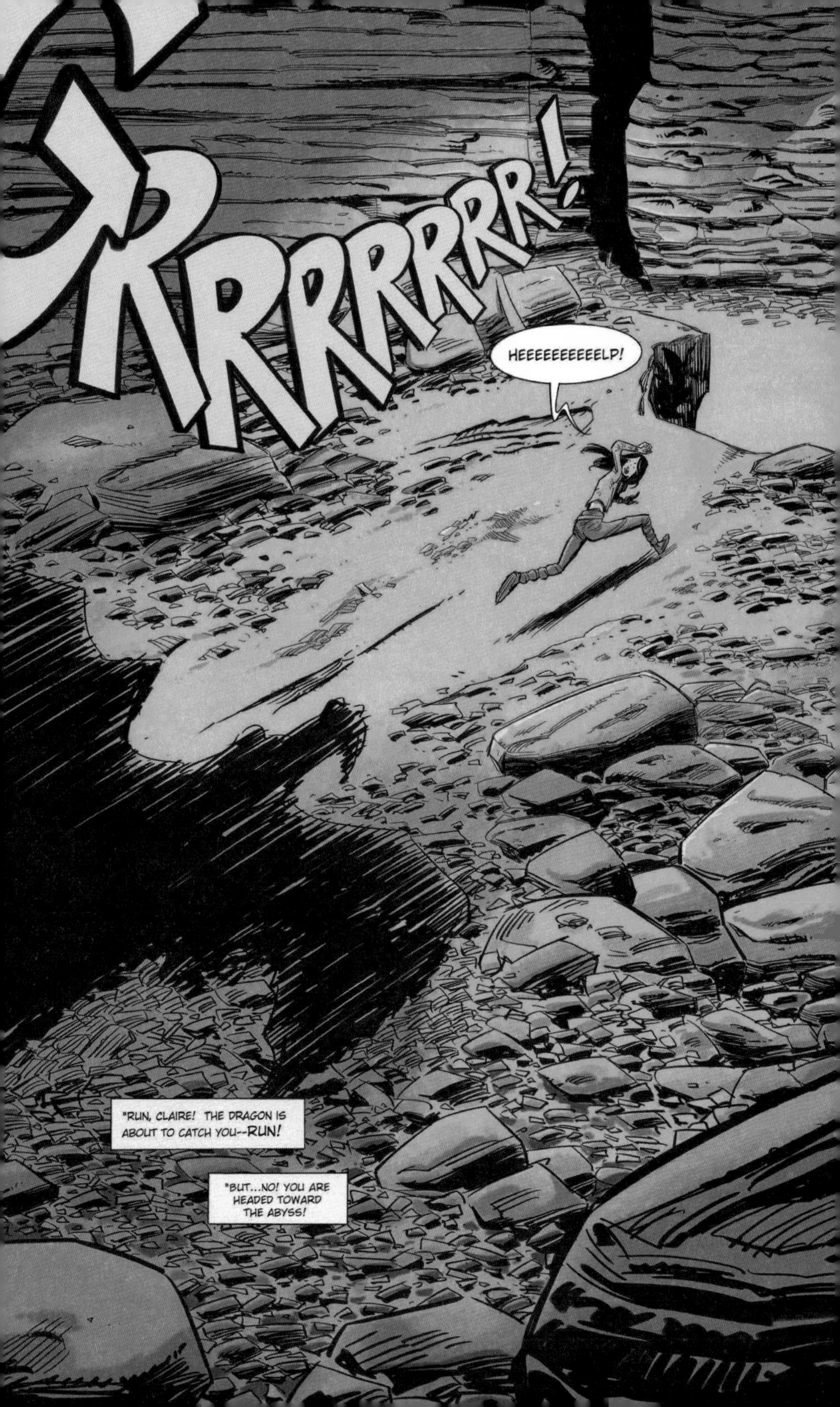
RRRRRRRR!
HEEEEEEEEEELP!
"RUN, CLAIRE! THE DRAGON IS ABOUT TO CATCH YOU--RUN!
"BUT...NO! YOU ARE HEADED TOWARD THE ABYSS!

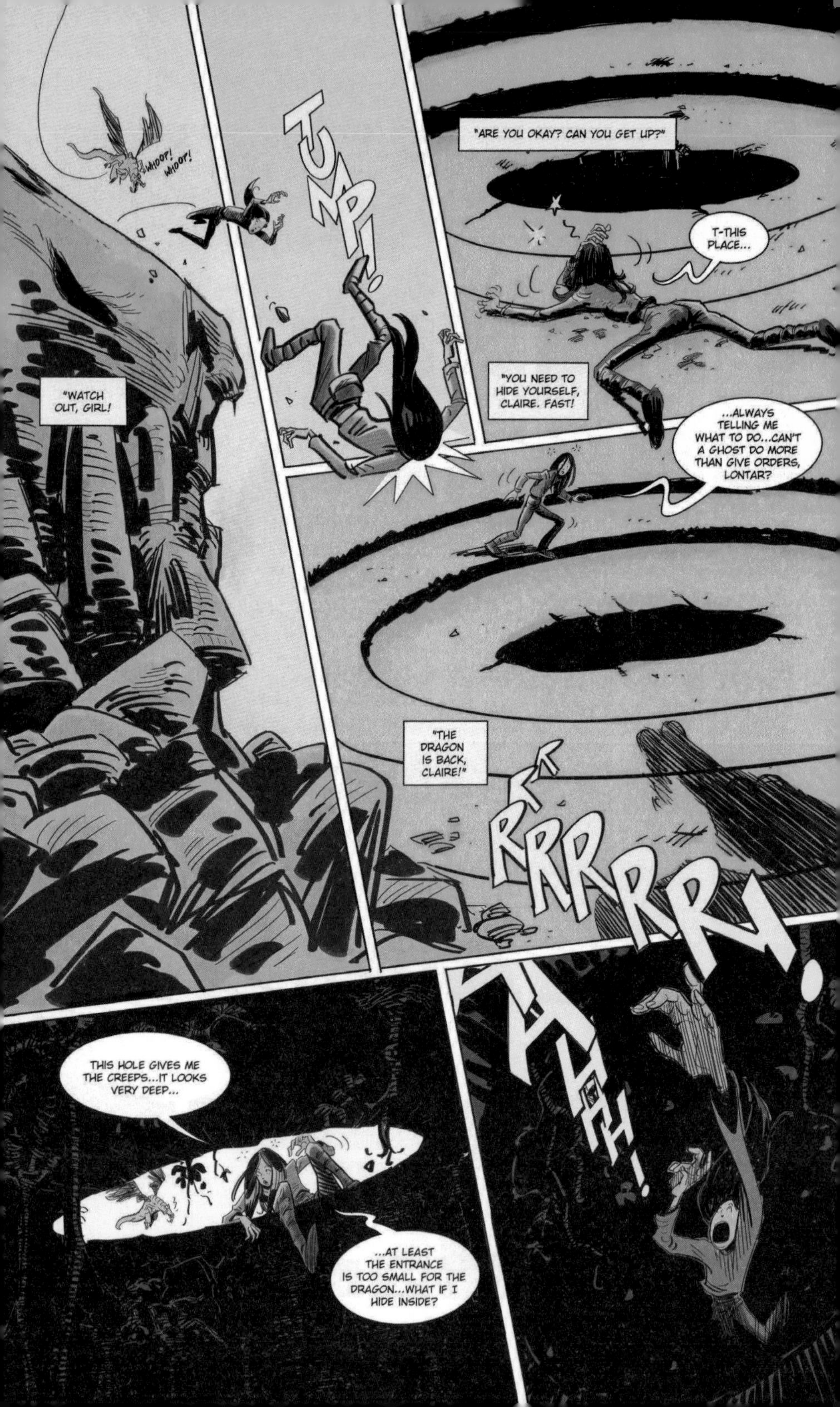

WHOOP! WHOOP!
"WATCH OUT, GIRL!
TUMP!
"ARE YOU OKAY? CAN YOU GET UP?"
T-THIS PLACE...
"YOU NEED TO HIDE YOURSELF, CLAIRE. FAST!
...ALWAYS TELLING ME WHAT TO DO...CAN'T A GHOST DO MORE THAN GIVE ORDERS, LONTAR?
"THE DRAGON IS BACK, CLAIRE!"
RRRRRR!
THIS HOLE GIVES ME THE CREEPS...IT LOOKS VERY DEEP...
...AT LEAST THE ENTRANCE IS TOO SMALL FOR THE DRAGON...WHAT IF I HIDE INSIDE?
AAHHH!

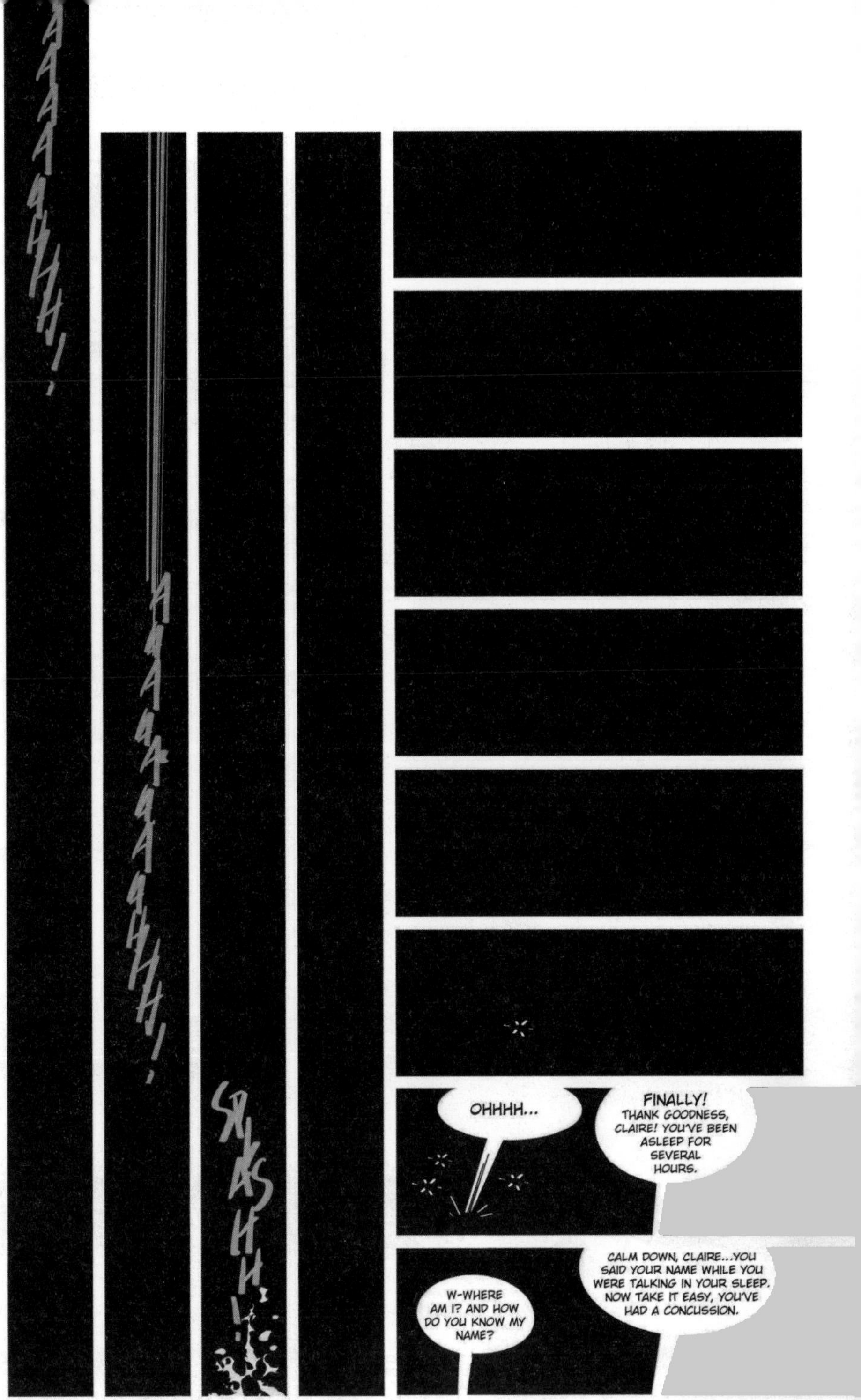
OHHHH...
FINALLY! THANK GOODNESS, CLAIRE! YOU'VE BEEN ASLEEP FOR SEVERAL HOURS.
W-WHERE AM I? AND HOW DO YOU KNOW MY NAME?
CALM DOWN, CLAIRE...YOU SAID YOUR NAME WHILE YOU WERE TALKING IN YOUR SLEEP. NOW TAKE IT EASY, YOU'VE HAD A CONCUSSION.

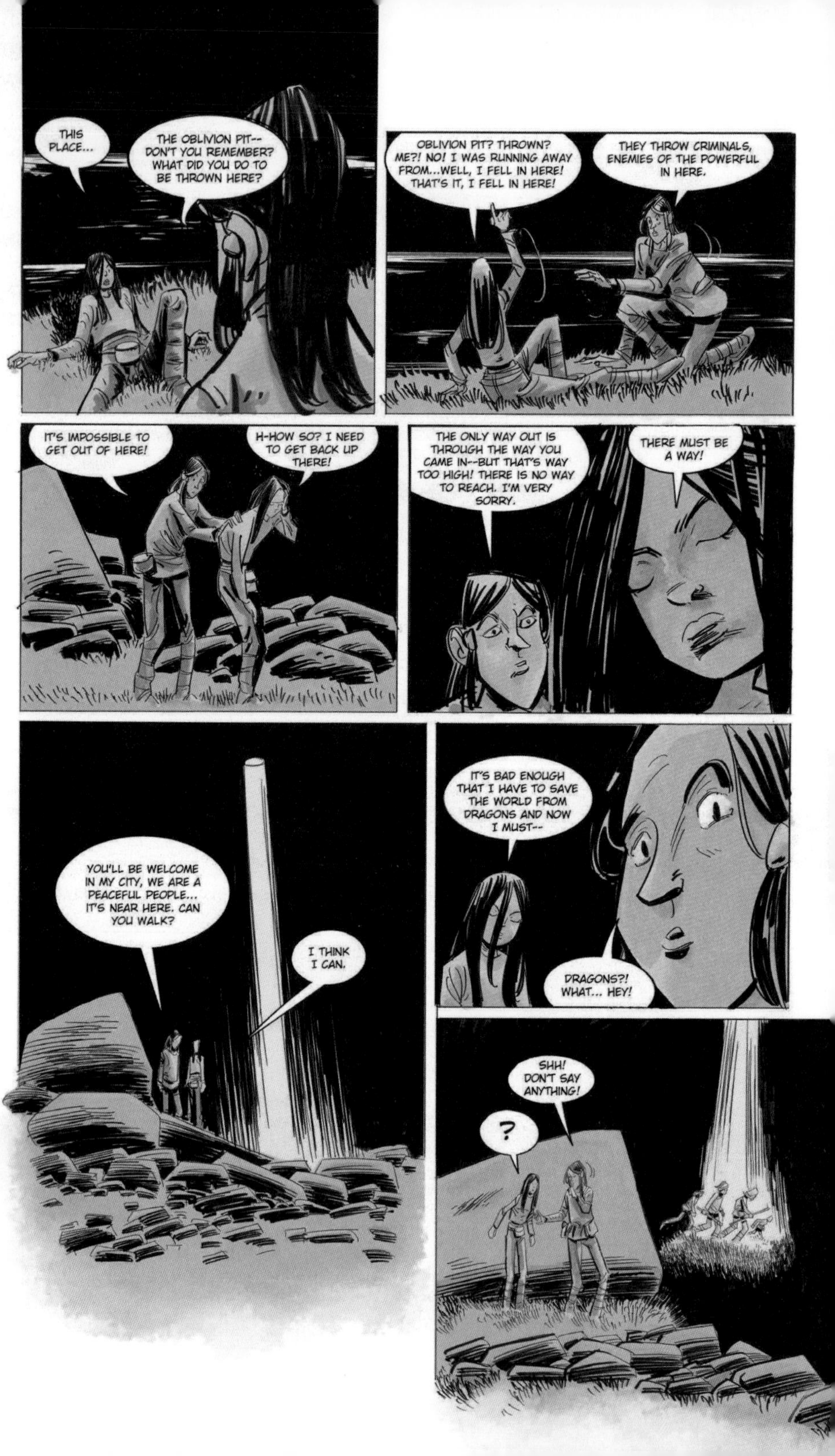

THIS PLACE...
THE OBLIVION PIT-- DON'T YOU REMEMBER? WHAT DID YOU DO TO BE THROWN HERE?
OBLIVION PIT? THROWN? ME?! NO! I WAS RUNNING AWAY FROM...WELL, I FELL IN HERE! THAT'S IT, I FELL IN HERE!
THEY THROW CRIMINALS, ENEMIES OF THE POWERFUL IN HERE.
IT'S IMPOSSIBLE TO GET OUT OF HERE!
H-HOW SO? I NEED TO GET BACK UP THERE!
THE ONLY WAY OUT IS THROUGH THE WAY YOU CAME IN--BUT THAT'S WAY TOO HIGH! THERE IS NO WAY TO REACH. I'M VERY SORRY.
THERE MUST BE A WAY!
YOU'LL BE WELCOME IN MY CITY, WE ARE A PEACEFUL PEOPLE... IT'S NEAR HERE. CAN YOU WALK?
I THINK I CAN.
IT'S BAD ENOUGH THAT I HAVE TO SAVE THE WORLD FROM DRAGONS AND NOW I MUST--
DRAGONS?! WHAT... HEY!
SHH! DON'T SAY ANYTHING!
?

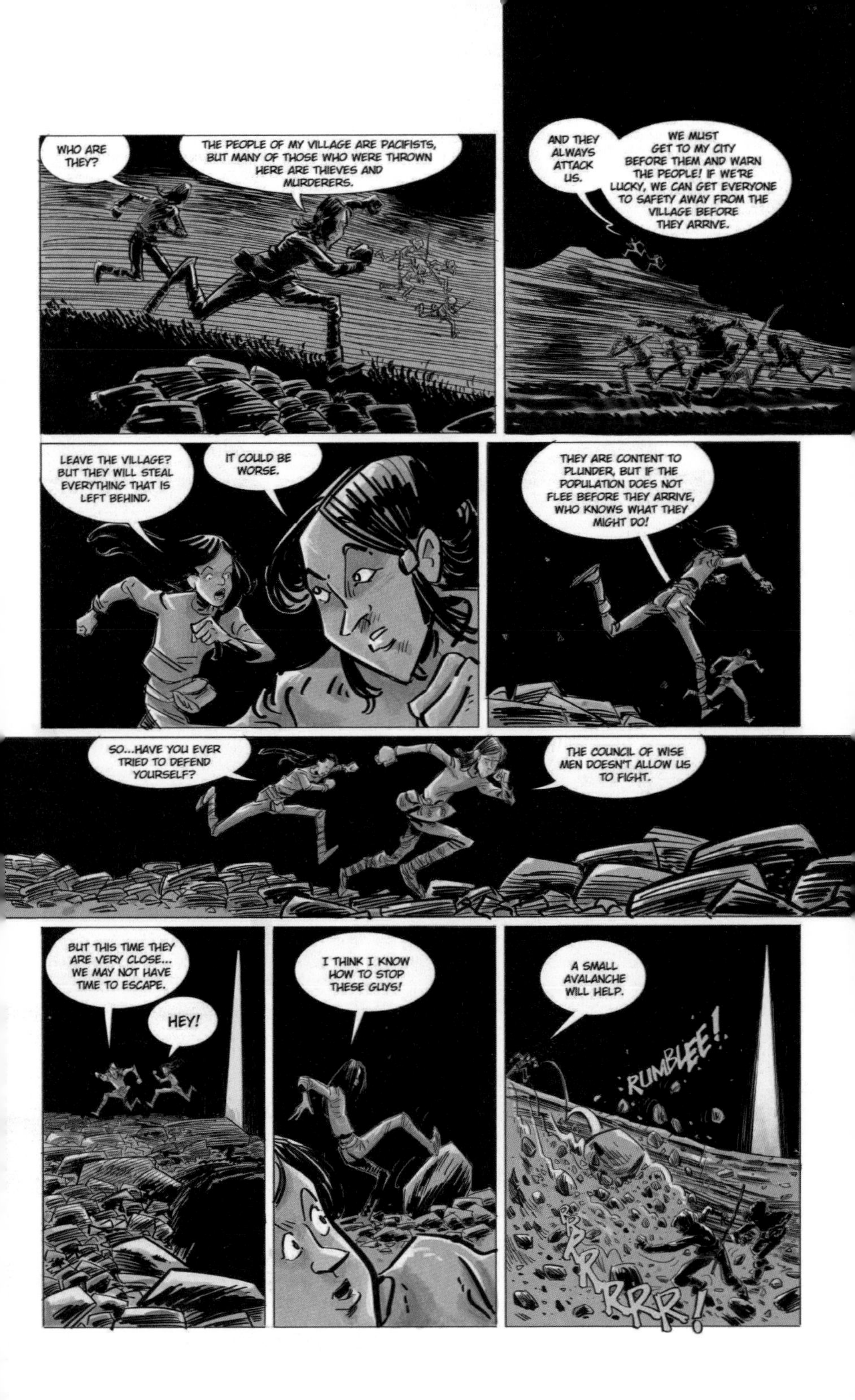
WHO ARE THEY?
THE PEOPLE OF MY VILLAGE ARE PACIFISTS, BUT MANY OF THOSE WHO WERE THROWN HERE ARE THIEVES AND MURDERERS.
AND THEY ALWAYS ATTACK US.
WE MUST GET TO MY CITY BEFORE THEM AND WARN THE PEOPLE! IF WE'RE LUCKY, WE CAN GET EVERYONE TO SAFETY AWAY FROM THE VILLAGE BEFORE THEY ARRIVE.
LEAVE THE VILLAGE? BUT THEY WILL STEAL EVERYTHING THAT IS LEFT BEHIND.
IT COULD BE WORSE.
THEY ARE CONTENT TO PLUNDER, BUT IF THE POPULATION DOES NOT FLEE BEFORE THEY ARRIVE, WHO KNOWS WHAT THEY MIGHT DO!
SO...HAVE YOU EVER TRIED TO DEFEND YOURSELF?
THE COUNCIL OF WISE MEN DOESN'T ALLOW US TO FIGHT.
BUT THIS TIME THEY ARE VERY CLOSE... WE MAY NOT HAVE TIME TO ESCAPE.
HEY!
I THINK I KNOW HOW TO STOP THESE GUYS!
A SMALL AVALANCHE WILL HELP.
RUMBLEE!
RRRRRR!

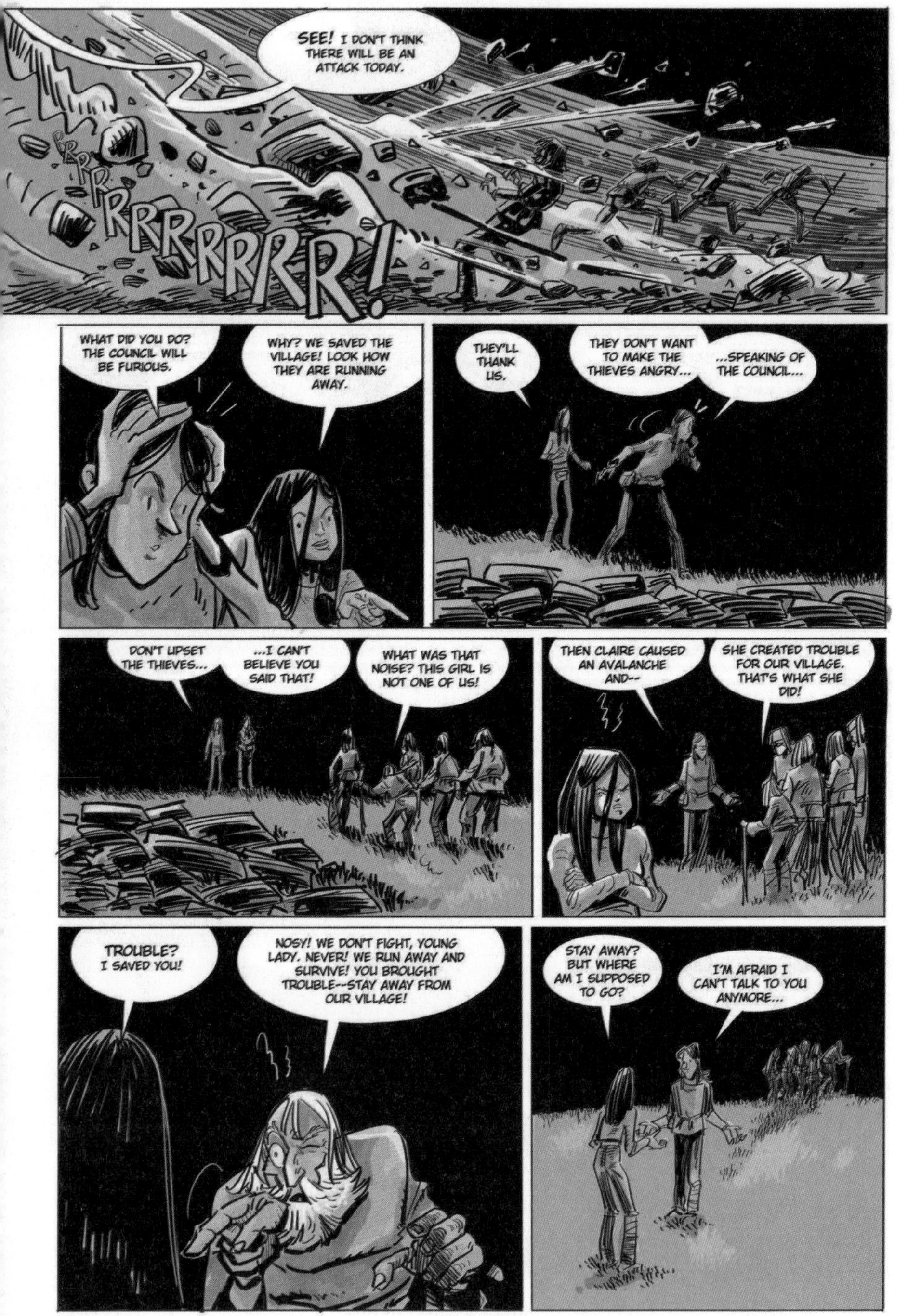
SEE! I DON'T THINK THERE WILL BE AN ATTACK TODAY.
RRRRRRRRRRRR!
WHAT DID YOU DO? THE COUNCIL WILL BE FURIOUS.
WHY? WE SAVED THE VILLAGE! LOOK HOW THEY ARE RUNNING AWAY.
THEY'LL THANK US.
THEY DON'T WANT TO MAKE THE THIEVES ANGRY...
...SPEAKING OF THE COUNCIL...
DON'T UPSET THE THIEVES...
...I CAN'T BELIEVE YOU SAID THAT!
WHAT WAS THAT NOISE? THIS GIRL IS NOT ONE OF US!
THEN CLAIRE CAUSED AN AVALANCHE AND--
SHE CREATED TROUBLE FOR OUR VILLAGE. THAT'S WHAT SHE DID!
TROUBLE? I SAVED YOU!
NOSY! WE DON'T FIGHT, YOUNG LADY. NEVER! WE RUN AWAY AND SURVIVE! YOU BROUGHT TROUBLE--STAY AWAY FROM OUR VILLAGE!
STAY AWAY? BUT WHERE AM I SUPPOSED TO GO?
I'M AFRAID I CAN'T TALK TO YOU ANYMORE...

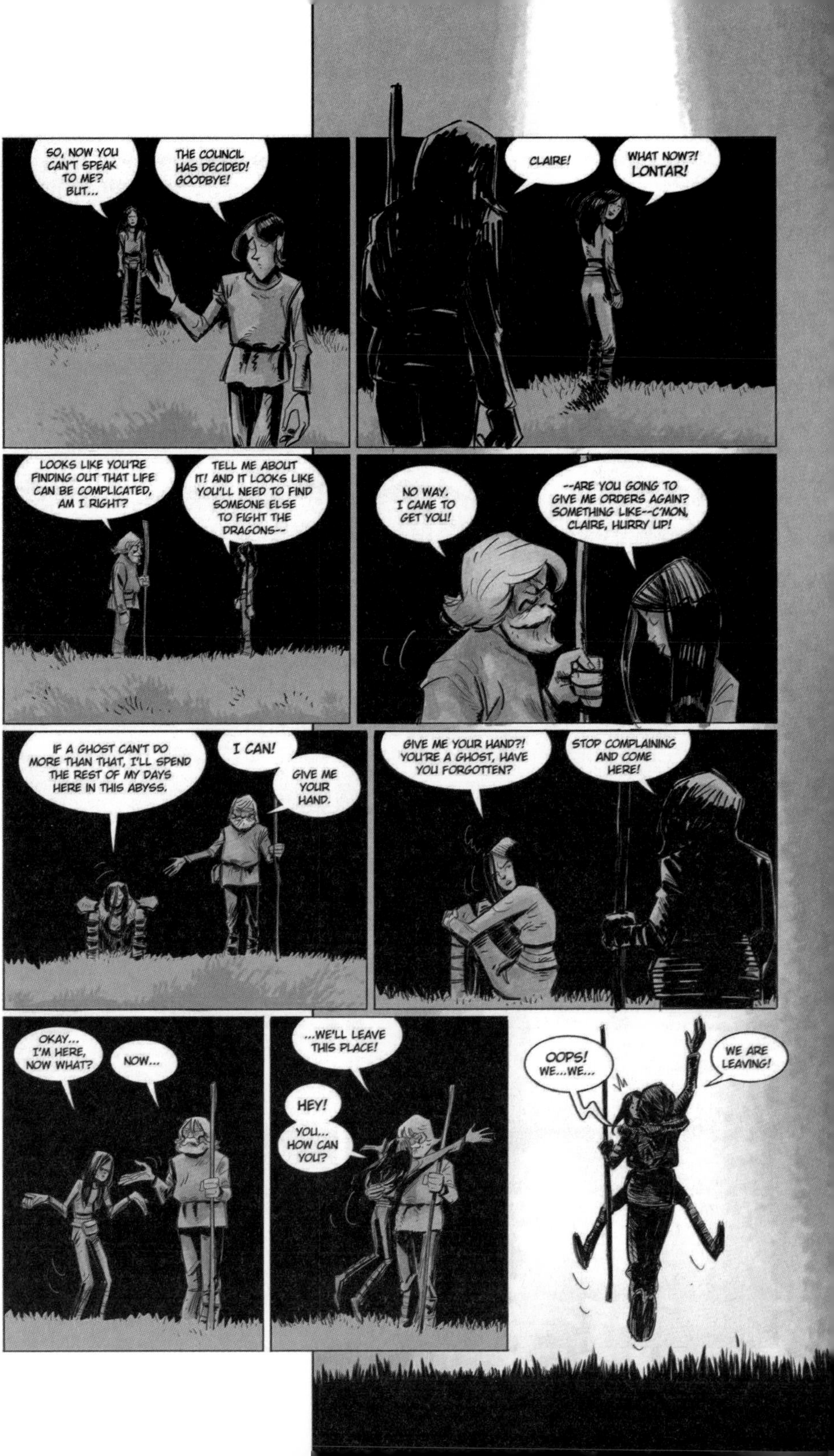
SO, NOW YOU CAN'T SPEAK TO ME? BUT...
THE COUNCIL HAS DECIDED! GOODBYE!
CLAIRE!
WHAT NOW?! LONTAR!
LOOKS LIKE YOU'RE FINDING OUT THAT LIFE CAN BE COMPLICATED, AM I RIGHT?
TELL ME ABOUT IT! AND IT LOOKS LIKE YOU'LL NEED TO FIND SOMEONE ELSE TO FIGHT THE DRAGONS--
NO WAY. I CAME TO GET YOU!
--ARE YOU GOING TO GIVE ME ORDERS AGAIN? SOMETHING LIKE--C'MON, CLAIRE, HURRY UP!
IF A GHOST CAN'T DO MORE THAN THAT, I'LL SPEND THE REST OF MY DAYS HERE IN THIS ABYSS.
I CAN!
GIVE ME YOUR HAND.
GIVE ME YOUR HAND?! YOU'RE A GHOST, HAVE YOU FORGOTTEN?
STOP COMPLAINING AND COME HERE!
OKAY... I'M HERE, NOW WHAT?
NOW...
...WE'LL LEAVE THIS PLACE!
HEY!
YOU... HOW CAN YOU?
OOPS! WE...WE...
WE ARE LEAVING!

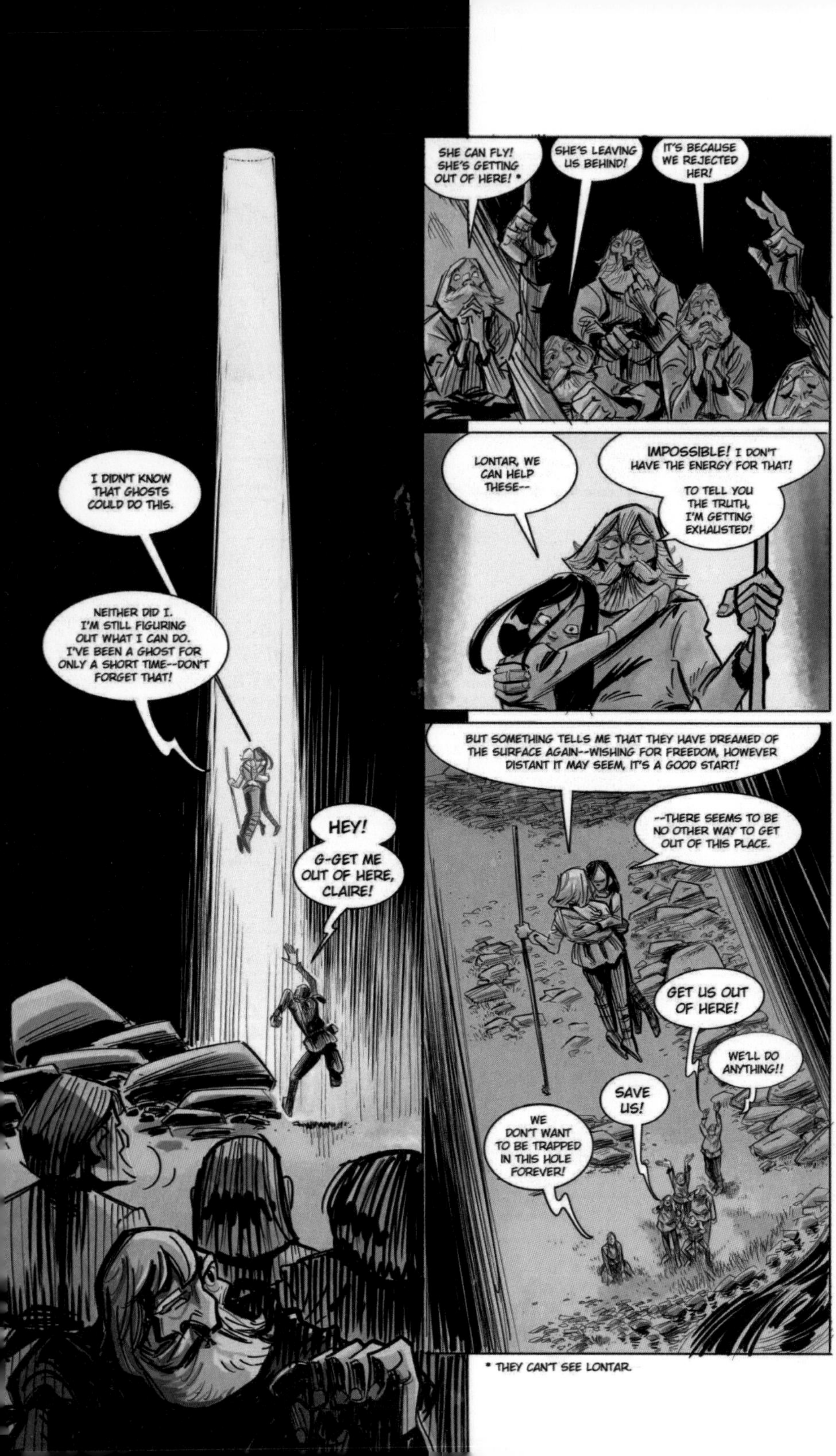
I DIDN'T KNOW THAT GHOSTS COULD DO THIS.
NEITHER DID I. I'M STILL FIGURING OUT WHAT I CAN DO. I'VE BEEN A GHOST FOR ONLY A SHORT TIME--DON'T FORGET THAT!
HEY!
G-GET ME OUT OF HERE, CLAIRE!
SHE CAN FLY! SHE'S GETTING OUT OF HERE! *
SHE'S LEAVING US BEHIND!
IT'S BECAUSE WE REJECTED HER!
LONTAR, WE CAN HELP THESE--
IMPOSSIBLE! I DON'T HAVE THE ENERGY FOR THAT!
TO TELL YOU THE TRUTH, I'M GETTING EXHAUSTED!
BUT SOMETHING TELLS ME THAT THEY HAVE DREAMED OF THE SURFACE AGAIN--WISHING FOR FREEDOM, HOWEVER DISTANT IT MAY SEEM, IT'S A GOOD START!
--THERE SEEMS TO BE NO OTHER WAY TO GET OUT OF THIS PLACE.
GET US OUT OF HERE!
WE'LL DO ANYTHING!!
SAVE US!
WE DON'T WANT TO BE TRAPPED IN THIS HOLE FOREVER!

* THEY CAN'T SEE LONTAR.

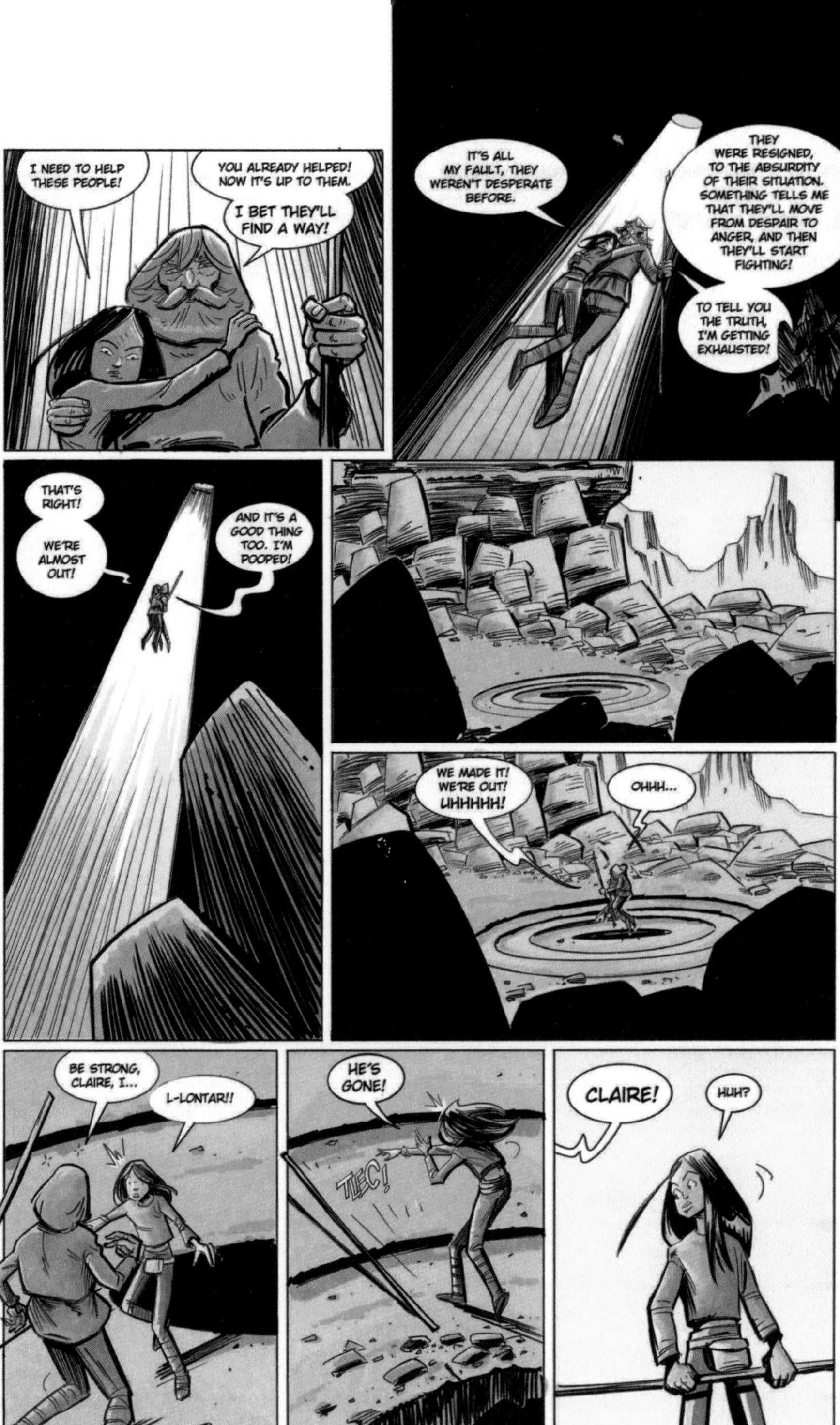
I NEED TO HELP THESE PEOPLE!
YOU ALREADY HELPED! NOW IT'S UP TO THEM.
I BET THEY'LL FIND A WAY!
IT'S ALL MY FAULT, THEY WEREN'T DESPERATE BEFORE.
THEY WERE RESIGNED, TO THE ABSURDITY OF THEIR SITUATION. SOMETHING TELLS ME THAT THEY'LL MOVE FROM DESPAIR TO ANGER, AND THEN THEY'LL START FIGHTING!
TO TELL YOU THE TRUTH, I'M GETTING EXHAUSTED!
THAT'S RIGHT!
WE'RE ALMOST OUT!
AND IT'S A GOOD THING TOO. I'M POOPED!
WE MADE IT! WE'RE OUT! UHHHHH!
OHHH...
BE STRONG, CLAIRE, I...
L-LONTAR!!
HE'S GONE!
TLEC!
CLAIRE!
HUH?

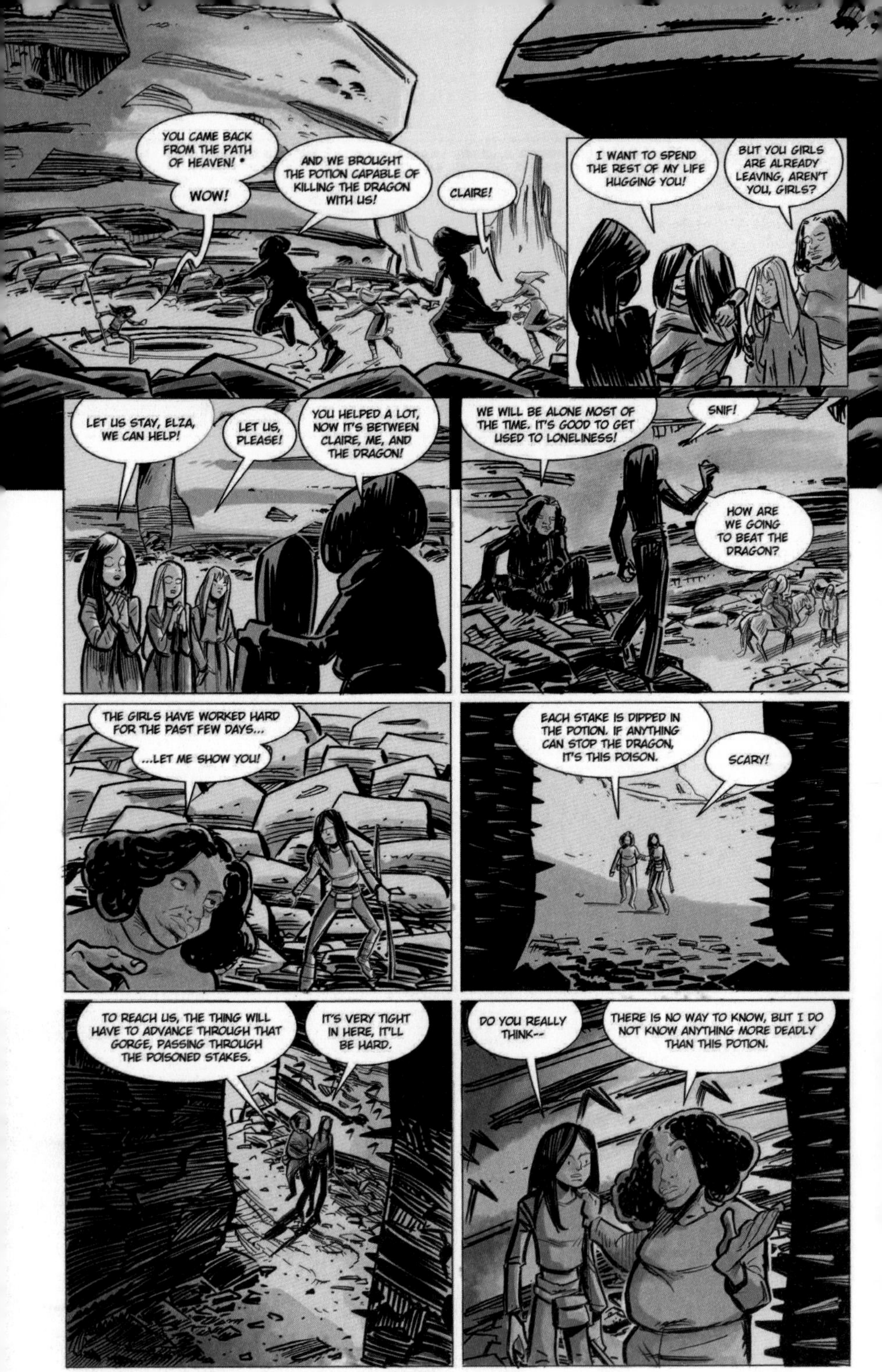
YOU CAME BACK FROM THE PATH OF HEAVEN! *
WOW!
AND WE BROUGHT THE POTION CAPABLE OF KILLING THE DRAGON WITH US!
CLAIRE!
I WANT TO SPEND THE REST OF MY LIFE HUGGING YOU!
BUT YOU GIRLS ARE ALREADY LEAVING, AREN'T YOU, GIRLS?
LET US STAY, ELZA, WE CAN HELP!
LET US, PLEASE!
YOU HELPED A LOT, NOW IT'S BETWEEN CLAIRE, ME, AND THE DRAGON!
WE WILL BE ALONE MOST OF THE TIME. IT'S GOOD TO GET USED TO LONELINESS!
SNIF!
HOW ARE WE GOING TO BEAT THE DRAGON?
THE GIRLS HAVE WORKED HARD FOR THE PAST FEW DAYS...
...LET ME SHOW YOU!
EACH STAKE IS DIPPED IN THE POTION. IF ANYTHING CAN STOP THE DRAGON, IT'S THIS POISON.
SCARY!
TO REACH US, THE THING WILL HAVE TO ADVANCE THROUGH THAT GORGE, PASSING THROUGH THE POISONED STAKES.
IT'S VERY TIGHT IN HERE, IT'LL BE HARD.
DO YOU REALLY THINK--
THERE IS NO WAY TO KNOW, BUT I DO NOT KNOW ANYTHING MORE DEADLY THAN THIS POTION.

* THE HIGHEST MOUNTAIN IN THE WORLD (SEE PREVIOUS EPISODE).

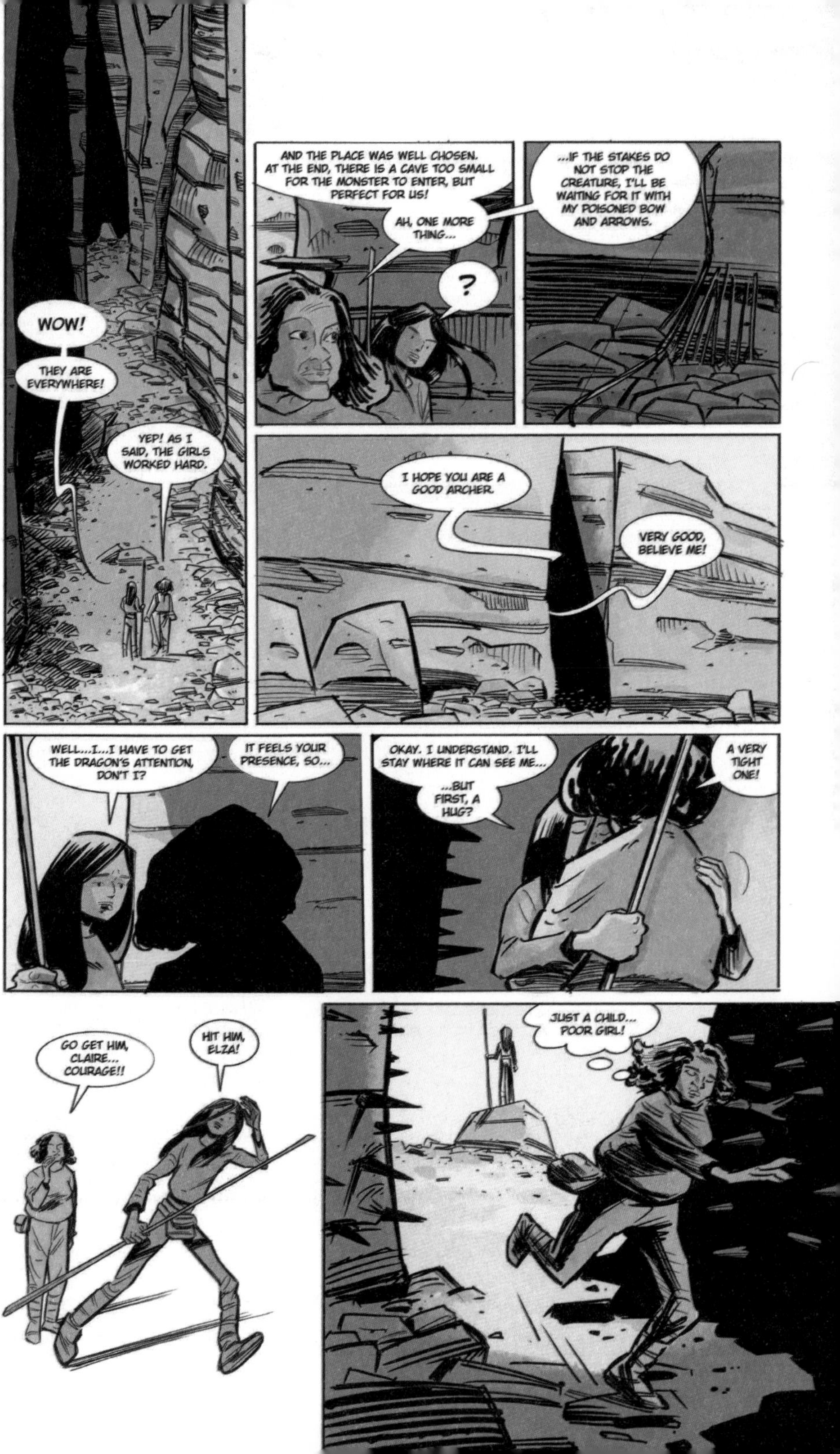
WOW!
THEY ARE EVERYWHERE!
YEP! AS I SAID, THE GIRLS WORKED HARD.
AND THE PLACE WAS WELL CHOSEN. AT THE END, THERE IS A CAVE TOO SMALL FOR THE MONSTER TO ENTER, BUT PERFECT FOR US!
AH, ONE MORE THING...
?
...IF THE STAKES DO NOT STOP THE CREATURE, I'LL BE WAITING FOR IT WITH MY POISONED BOW AND ARROWS.
I HOPE YOU ARE A GOOD ARCHER.
VERY GOOD, BELIEVE ME!
WELL...I...I HAVE TO GET THE DRAGON'S ATTENTION, DON'T I?
IT FEELS YOUR PRESENCE, SO...
OKAY. I UNDERSTAND. I'LL STAY WHERE IT CAN SEE ME...
...BUT FIRST, A HUG?
A VERY TIGHT ONE!
GO GET HIM, CLAIRE... COURAGE!!
HIT HIM, ELZA!
JUST A CHILD... POOR GIRL!

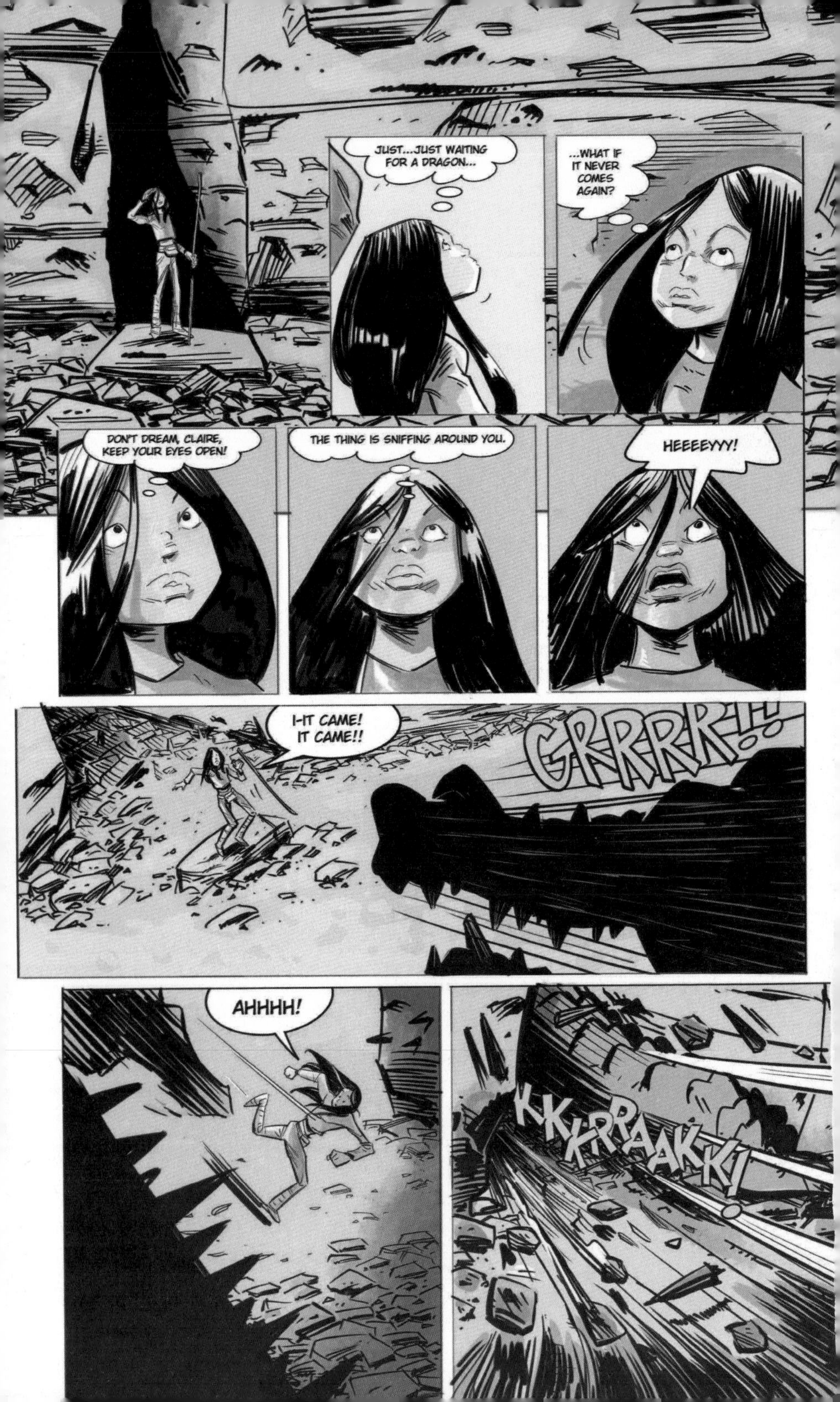

JUST...JUST WAITING FOR A DRAGON...
...WHAT IF IT NEVER COMES AGAIN?
DON'T DREAM, CLAIRE, KEEP YOUR EYES OPEN!
THE THING IS SNIFFING AROUND YOU.
HEEEEYYY!
I-IT CAME! IT CAME!!
GRRRR!!
AHHHH!
KKKRRAAKK!

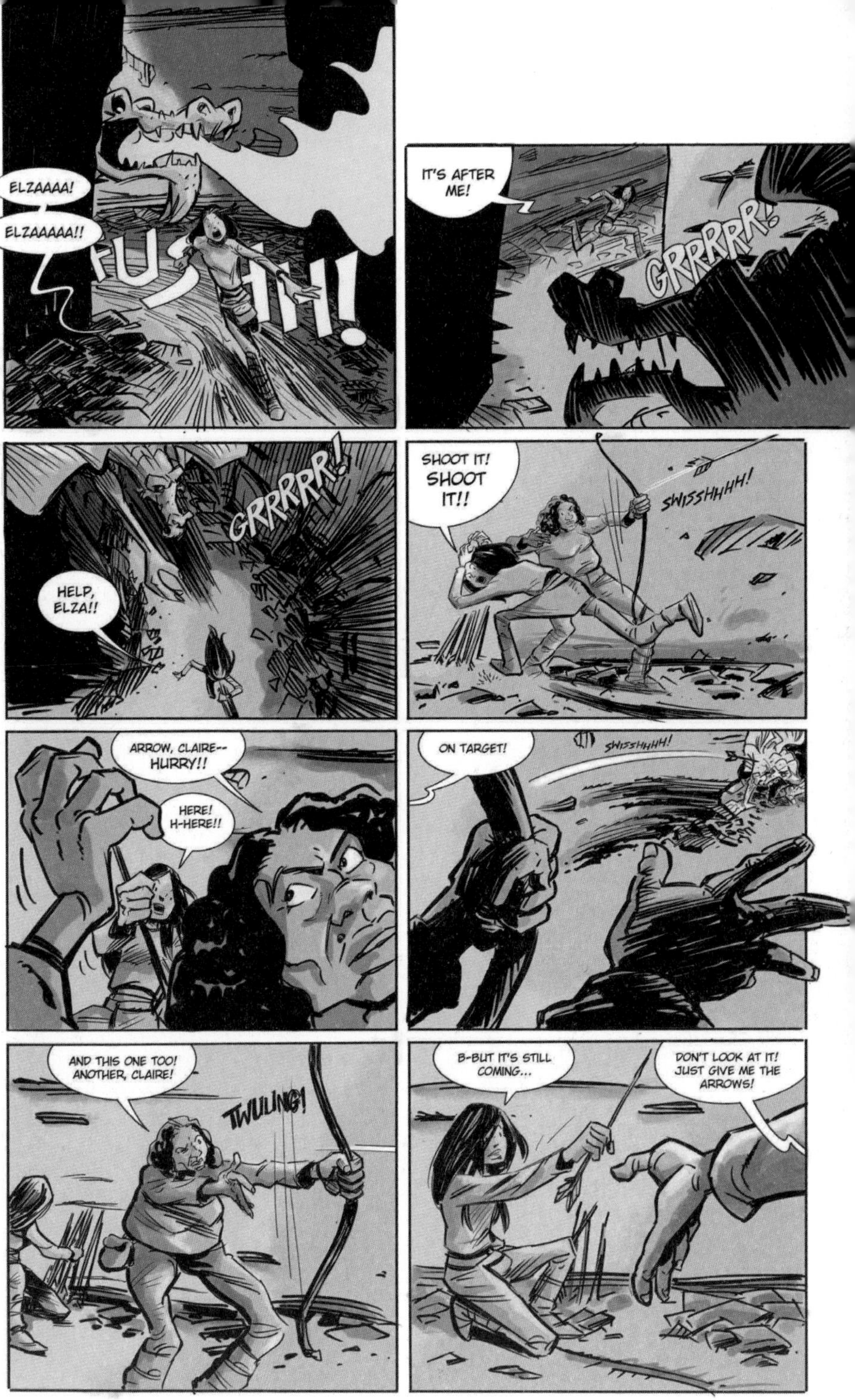
ELZAAAA!
ELZAAAAA!!
FUSHHH!
IT'S AFTER ME!
GRRRRR!
GRRRRR!
HELP, ELZA!!
SHOOT IT! SHOOT IT!!
SWISSHHHH!
ARROW, CLAIRE-- HURRY!!
HERE! H-HERE!!
ON TARGET!
SWISSHHHH!
AND THIS ONE TOO! ANOTHER, CLAIRE!
TWUUNG!
B-BUT IT'S STILL COMING...
DON'T LOOK AT IT! JUST GIVE ME THE ARROWS!

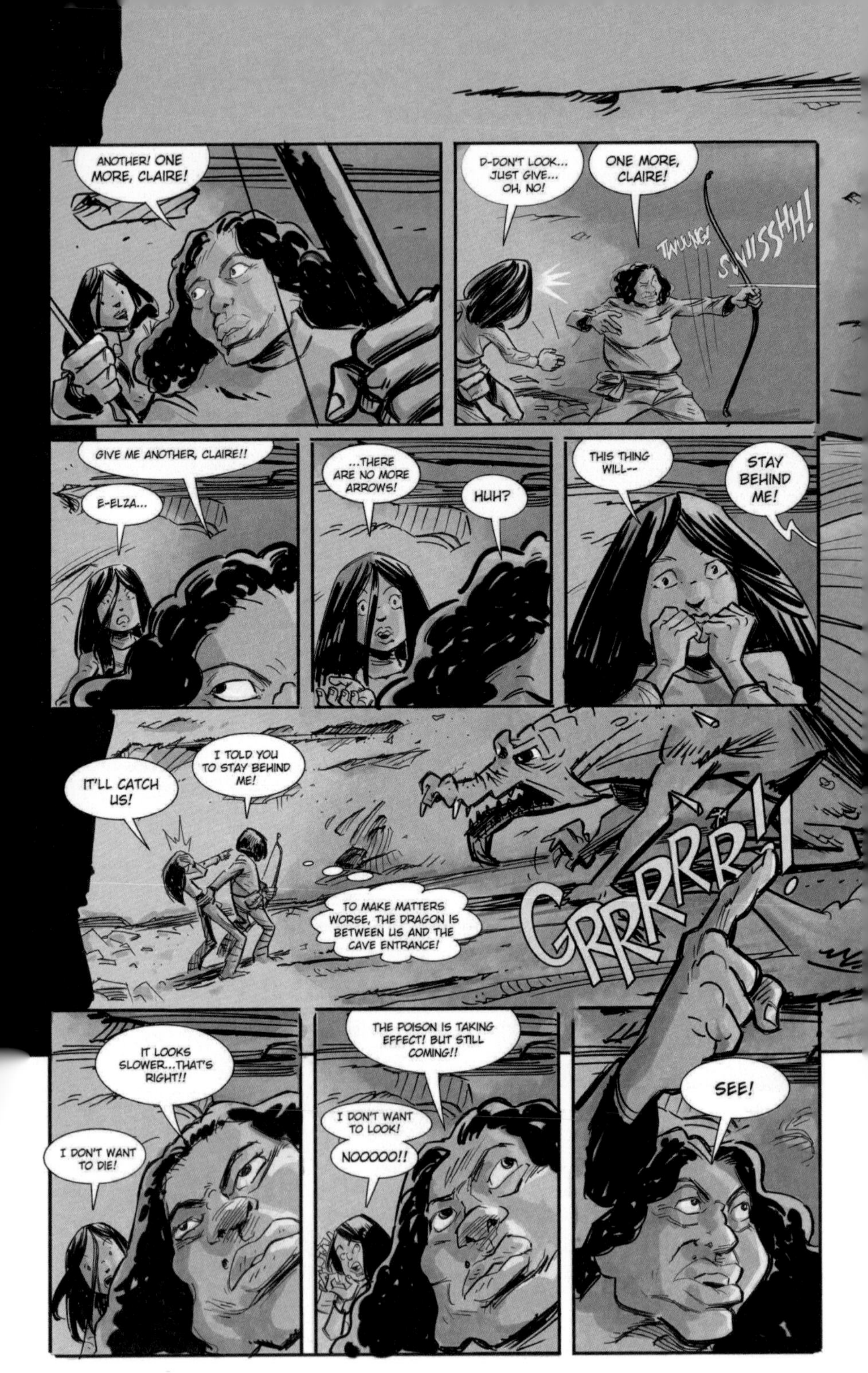

ANOTHER! ONE MORE, CLAIRE!
D-DON'T LOOK... JUST GIVE... OH, NO!
ONE MORE, CLAIRE!
TWUUNG!
SWIISSHH!
GIVE ME ANOTHER, CLAIRE!!
E-ELZA...
...THERE ARE NO MORE ARROWS!
HUH?
THIS THING WILL--
STAY BEHIND ME!
IT'LL CATCH US!
I TOLD YOU TO STAY BEHIND ME!
TO MAKE MATTERS WORSE, THE DRAGON IS BETWEEN US AND THE CAVE ENTRANCE!
GRRRRR!!
IT LOOKS SLOWER...THAT'S RIGHT!!
I DON'T WANT TO DIE!
THE POISON IS TAKING EFFECT! BUT STILL COMING!!
I DON'T WANT TO LOOK!
NOOOOO!!
SEE!

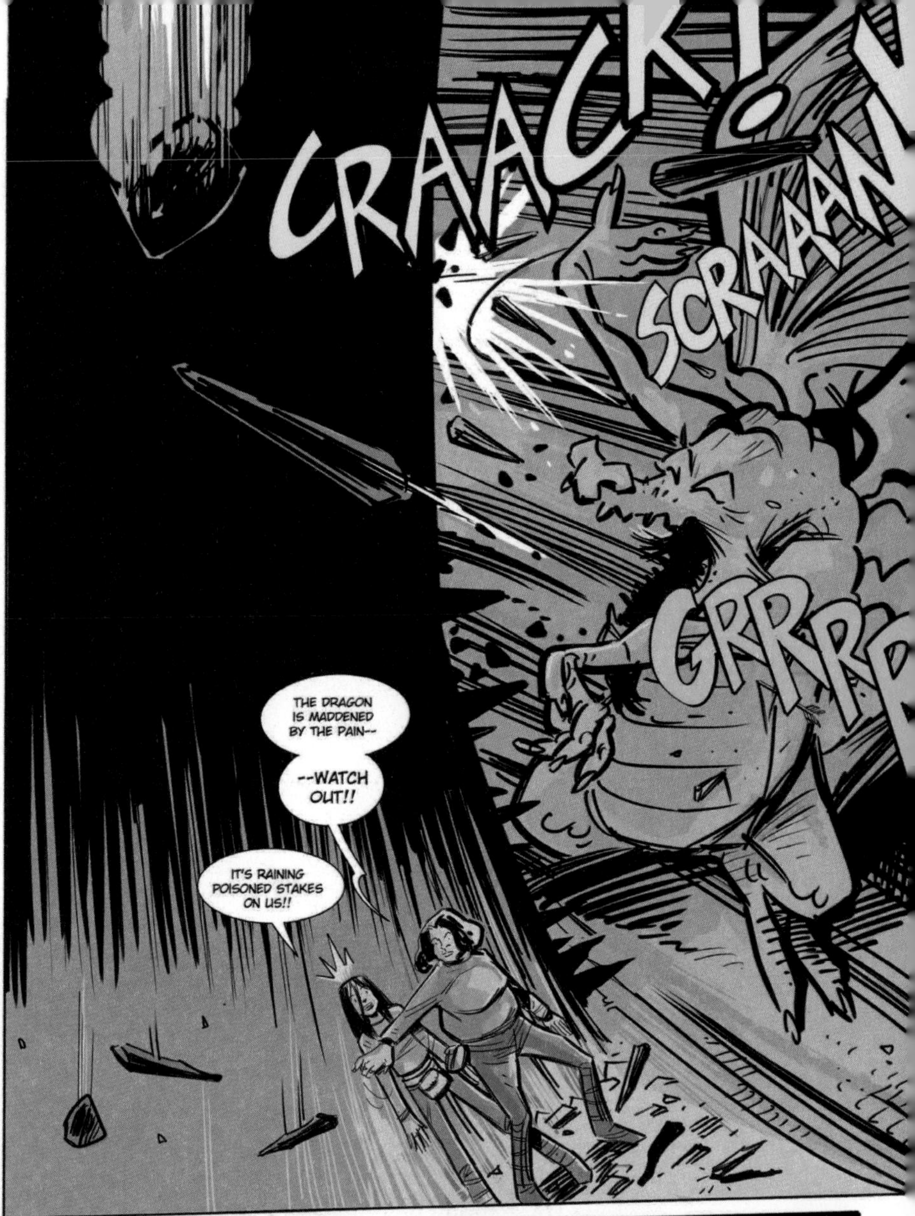
CRAACK!
SCRAAAN
GRRR
THE DRAGON IS MADDENED BY THE PAIN--
--WATCH OUT!!
IT'S RAINING POISONED STAKES ON US!!

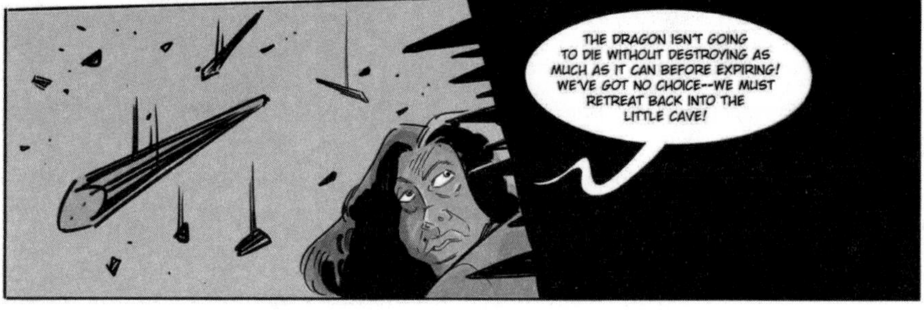
THE DRAGON ISN'T GOING TO DIE WITHOUT DESTROYING AS MUCH AS IT CAN BEFORE EXPIRING! WE'VE GOT NO CHOICE--WE MUST RETREAT BACK INTO THE LITTLE CAVE!

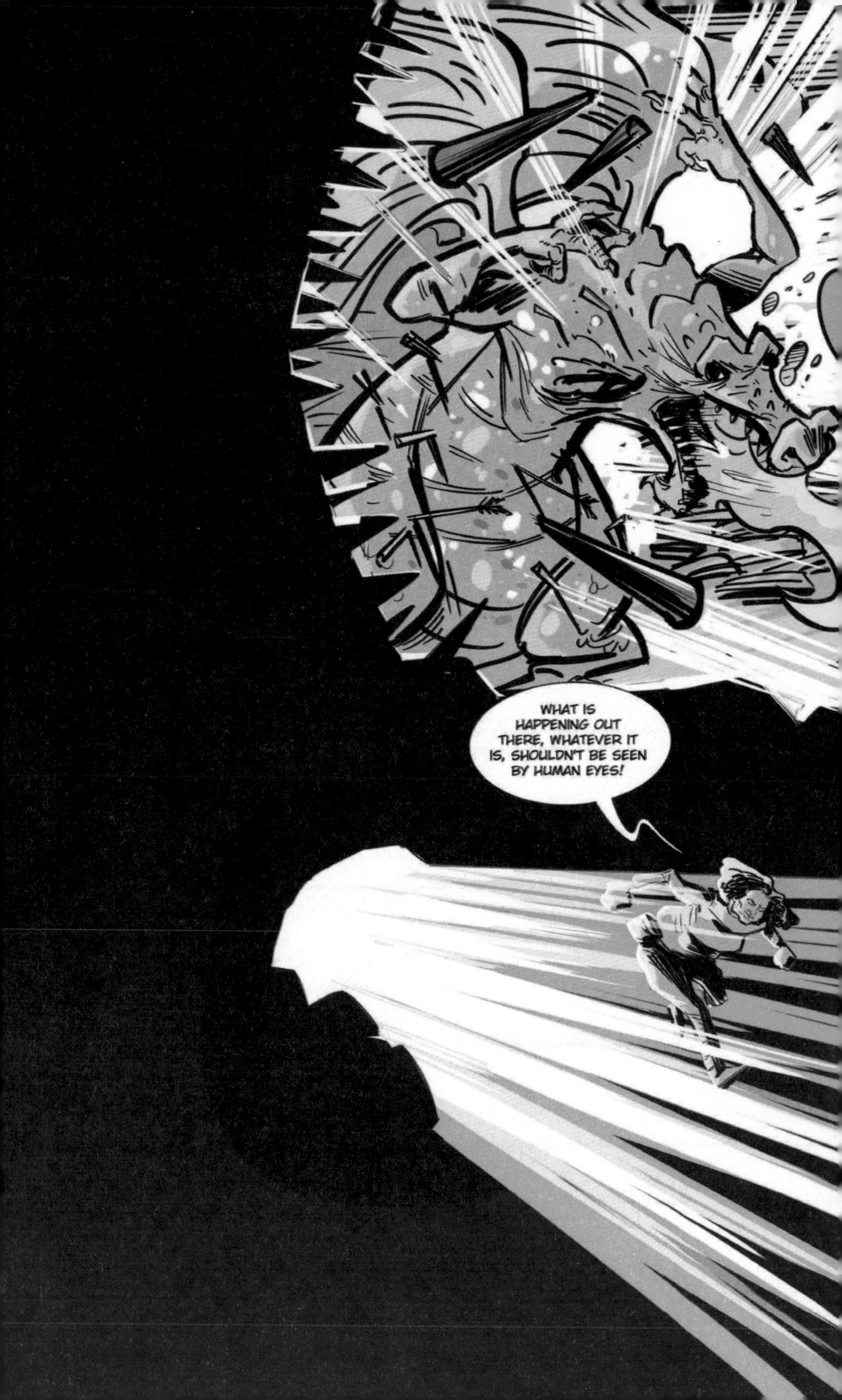
WHAT IS HAPPENING OUT THERE, WHATEVER IT IS, SHOULDN'T BE SEEN BY HUMAN EYES!

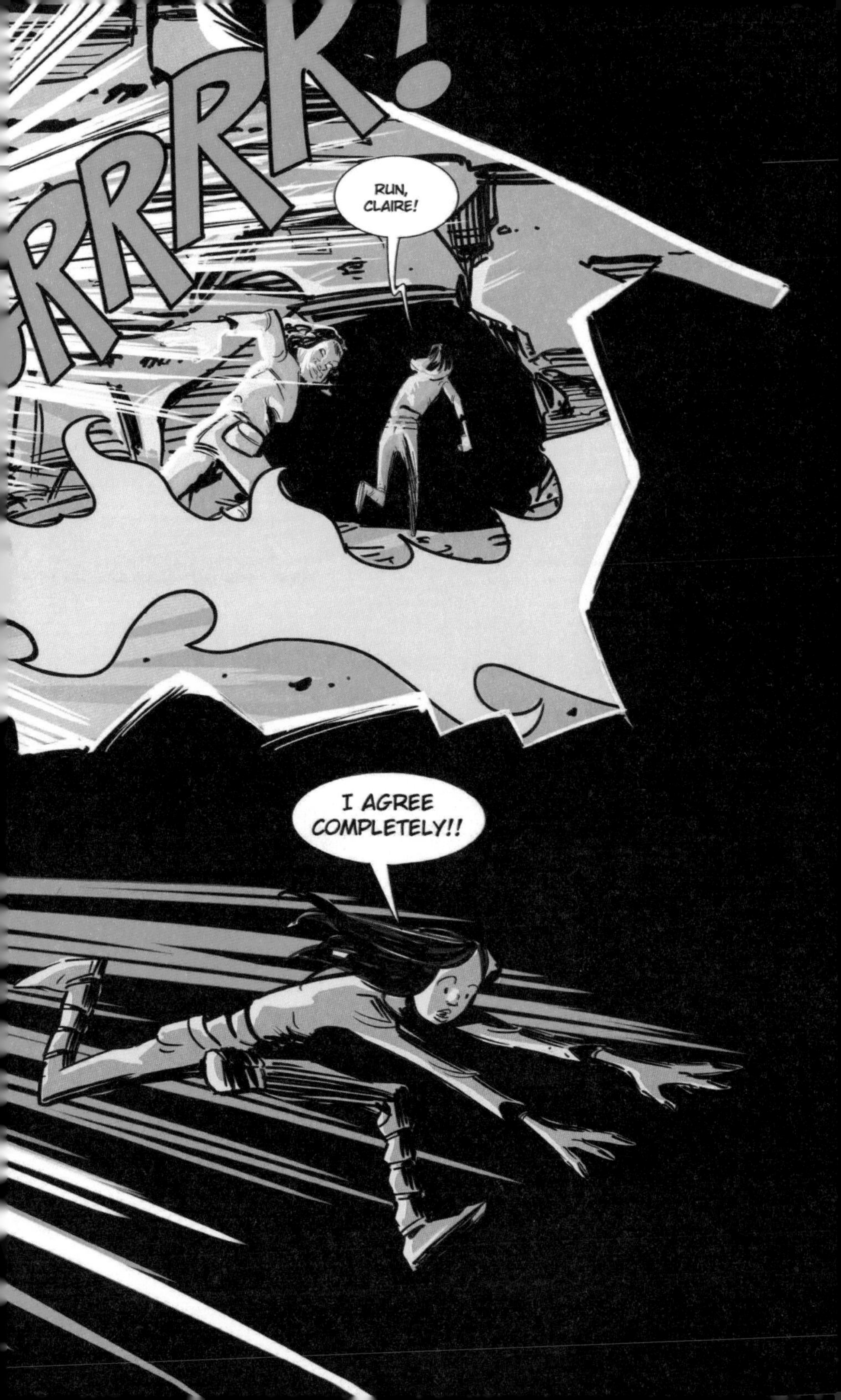
RRRRK!
RUN, CLAIRE!
I AGREE COMPLETELY!!

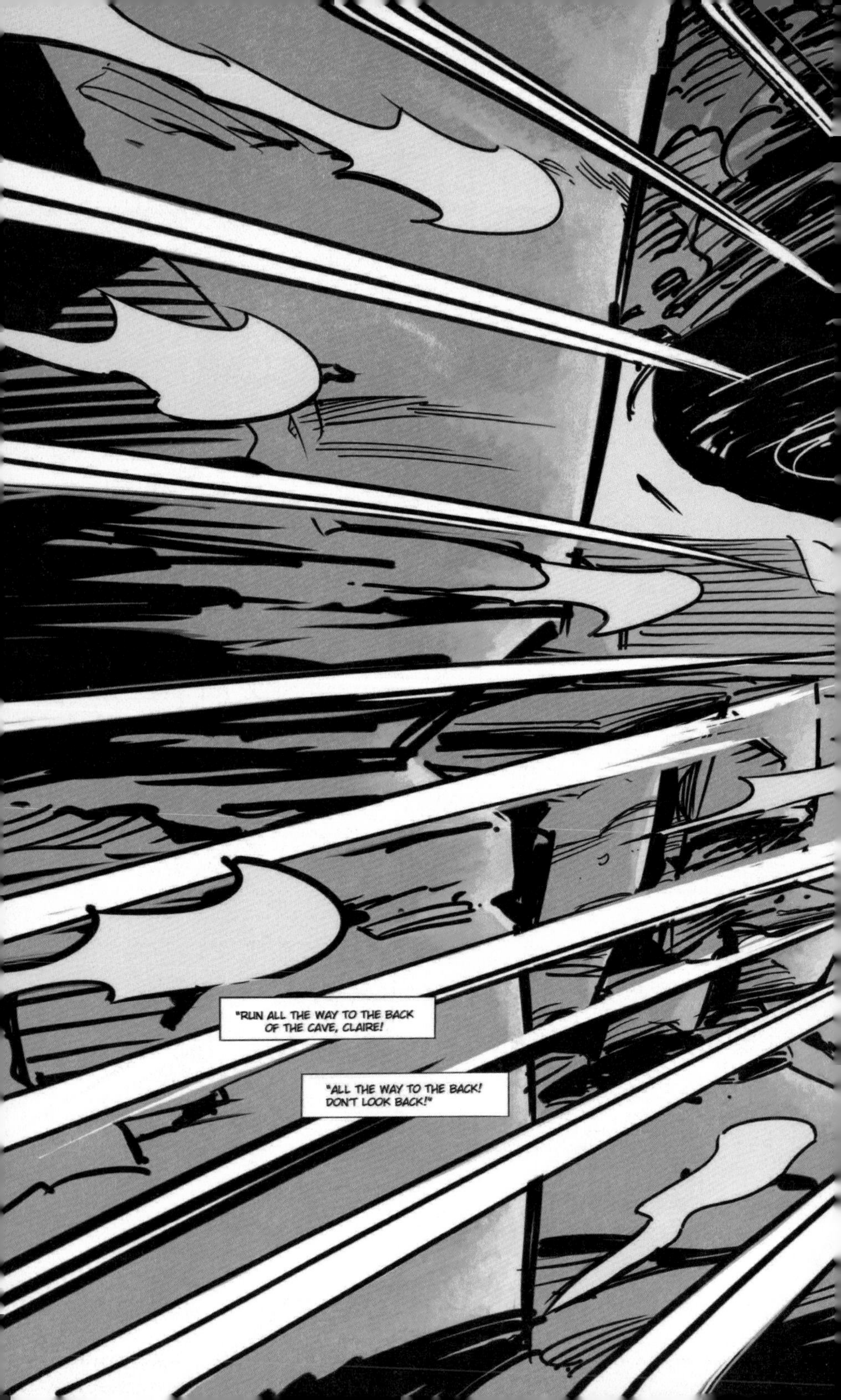
"RUN ALL THE WAY TO THE BACK
OF THE CAVE, CLAIRE!
"ALL THE WAY TO THE BACK!
DON'T LOOK BACK!"

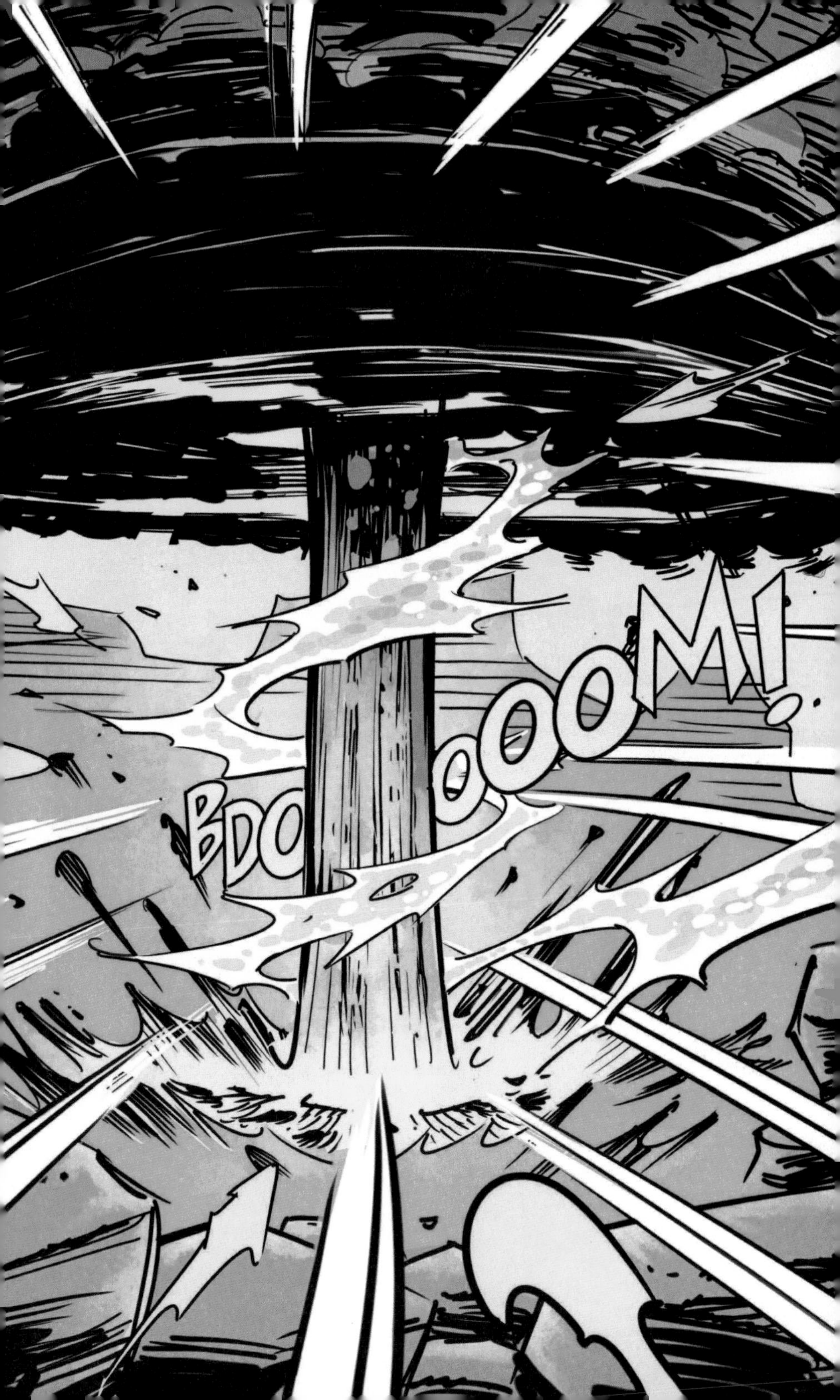
BDOOOOOM!

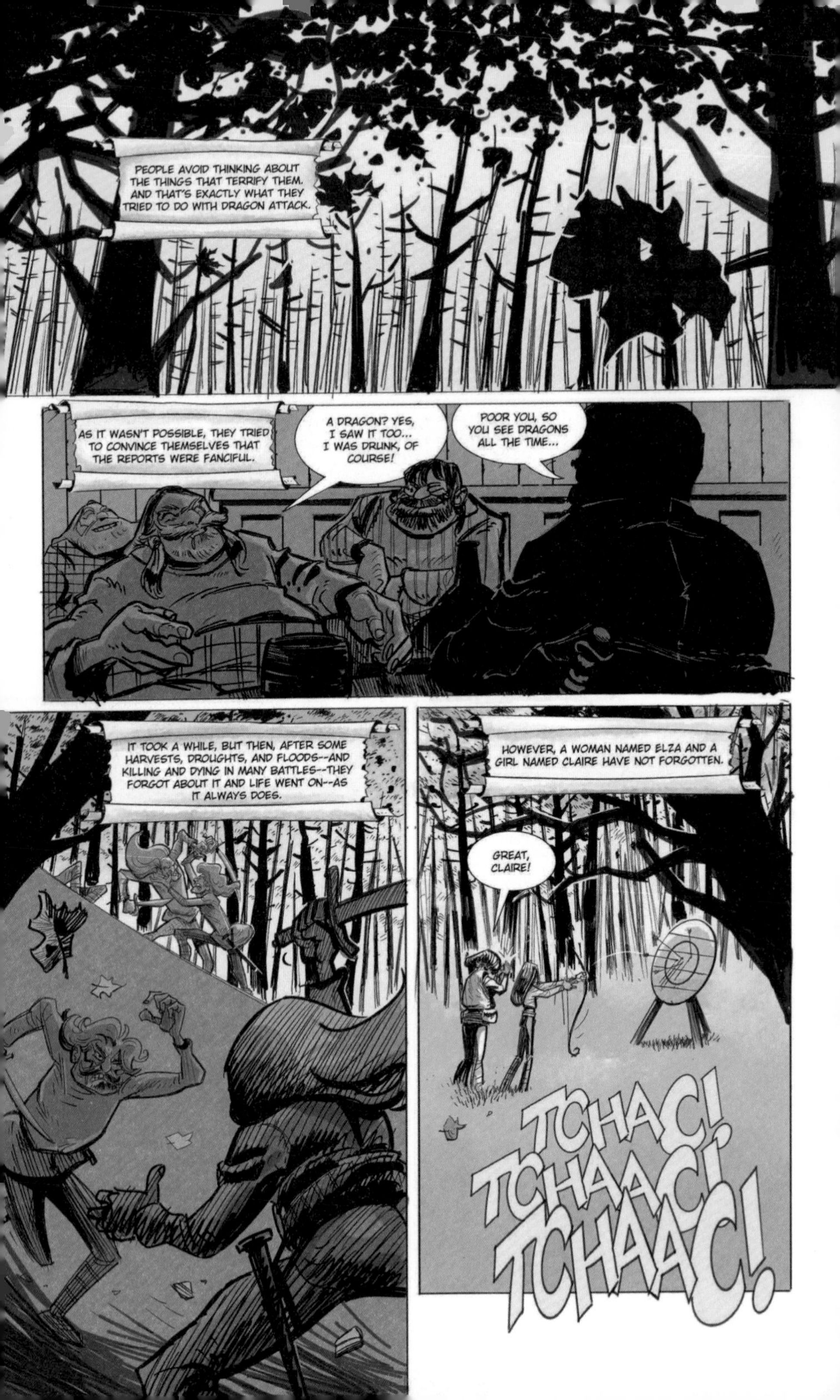
PEOPLE AVOID THINKING ABOUT THE THINGS THAT TERRIFY THEM, AND THAT'S EXACTLY WHAT THEY TRIED TO DO WITH DRAGON ATTACK.
AS IT WASN'T POSSIBLE, THEY TRIED TO CONVINCE THEMSELVES THAT THE REPORTS WERE FANCIFUL.
A DRAGON? YES, I SAW IT TOO... I WAS DRUNK, OF COURSE!
POOR YOU, SO YOU SEE DRAGONS ALL THE TIME...
IT TOOK A WHILE, BUT THEN, AFTER SOME HARVESTS, DROUGHTS, AND FLOODS--AND KILLING AND DYING IN MANY BATTLES--THEY FORGOT ABOUT IT AND LIFE WENT ON--AS IT ALWAYS DOES.
HOWEVER, A WOMAN NAMED ELZA AND A GIRL NAMED CLAIRE HAVE NOT FORGOTTEN.
GREAT, CLAIRE!
TCHAC! TCHAAC! TCHAAC!

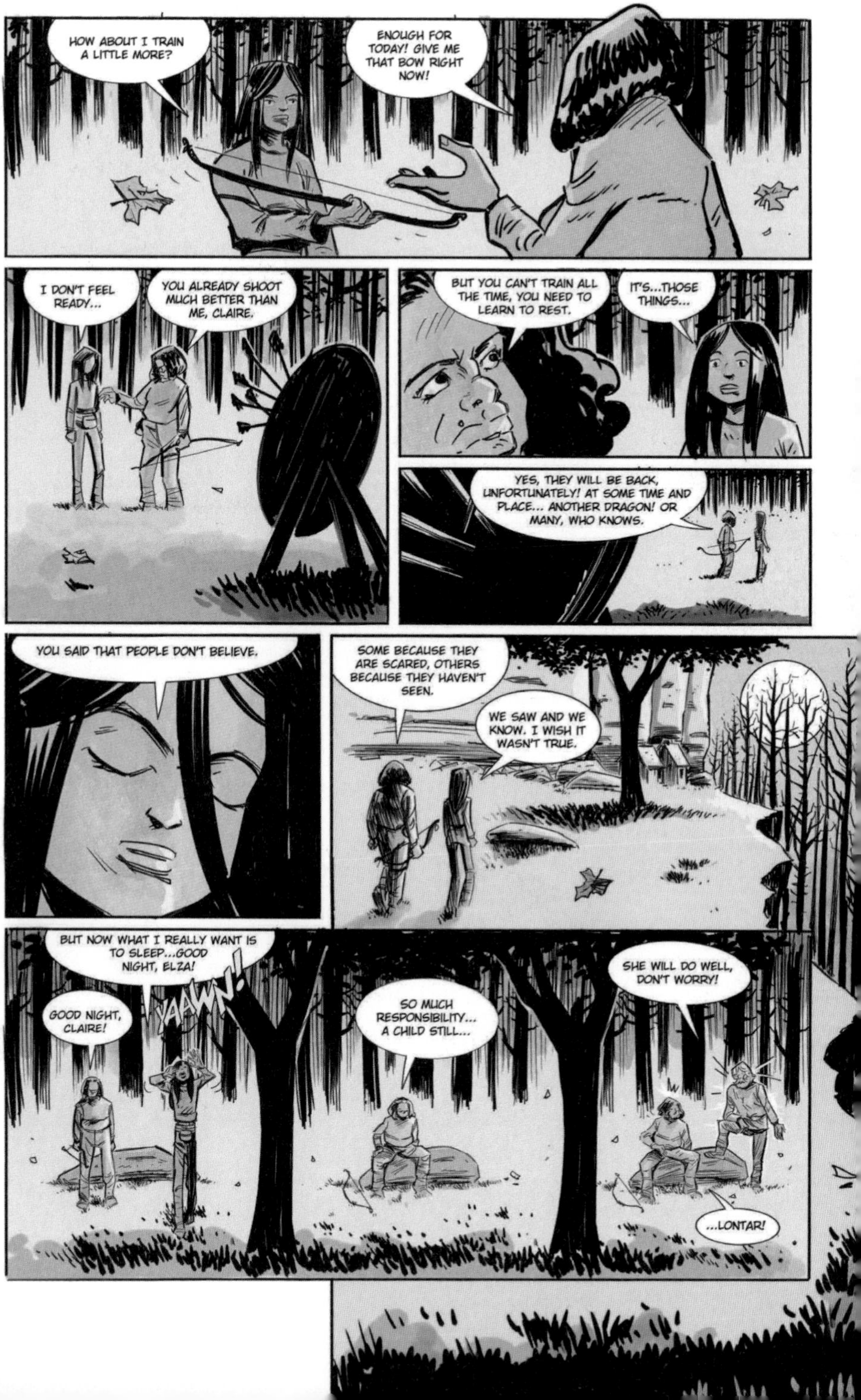
HOW ABOUT I TRAIN A LITTLE MORE?
ENOUGH FOR TODAY! GIVE ME THAT BOW RIGHT NOW!
I DON'T FEEL READY...
YOU ALREADY SHOOT MUCH BETTER THAN ME, CLAIRE.
BUT YOU CAN'T TRAIN ALL THE TIME, YOU NEED TO LEARN TO REST.
IT'S...THOSE THINGS...
YES, THEY WILL BE BACK, UNFORTUNATELY! AT SOME TIME AND PLACE... ANOTHER DRAGON! OR MANY, WHO KNOWS.
YOU SAID THAT PEOPLE DON'T BELIEVE.
SOME BECAUSE THEY ARE SCARED, OTHERS BECAUSE THEY HAVEN'T SEEN.
WE SAW AND WE KNOW. I WISH IT WASN'T TRUE.
BUT NOW WHAT I REALLY WANT IS TO SLEEP...GOOD NIGHT, ELZA!
YAAWN!
GOOD NIGHT, CLAIRE!
SO MUCH RESPONSIBILITY... A CHILD STILL...
SHE WILL DO WELL, DON'T WORRY!
...LONTAR!

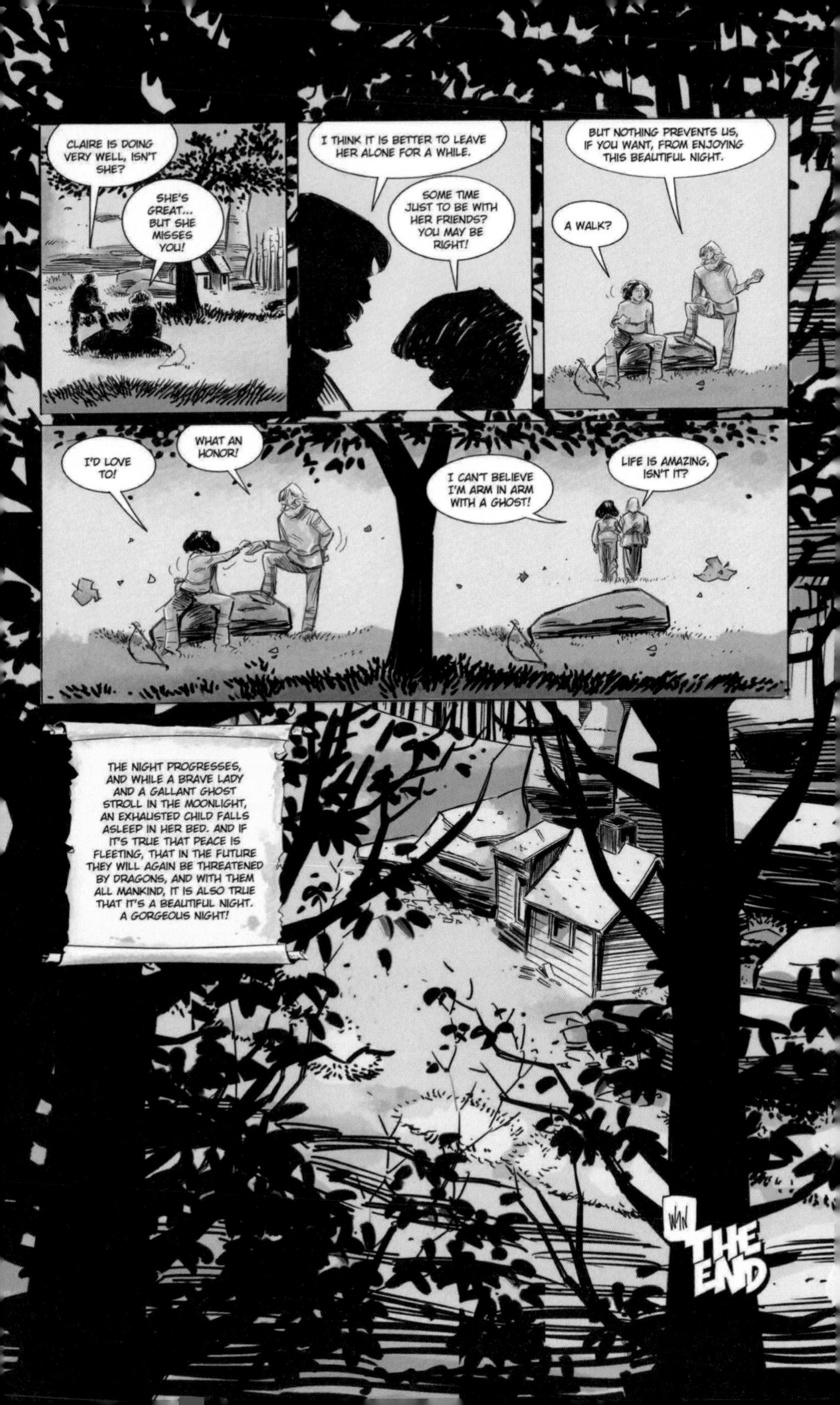

CLAIRE IS DOING VERY WELL, ISN'T SHE?
SHE'S GREAT... BUT SHE MISSES YOU!
I THINK IT IS BETTER TO LEAVE HER ALONE FOR A WHILE.
SOME TIME JUST TO BE WITH HER FRIENDS? YOU MAY BE RIGHT!
BUT NOTHING PREVENTS US, IF YOU WANT, FROM ENJOYING THIS BEAUTIFUL NIGHT.
A WALK?
I'D LOVE TO!
WHAT AN HONOR!
I CAN'T BELIEVE I'M ARM IN ARM WITH A GHOST!
LIFE IS AMAZING, ISN'T IT?
THE NIGHT PROGRESSES, AND WHILE A BRAVE LADY AND A GALLANT GHOST STROLL IN THE MOONLIGHT, AN EXHAUSTED CHILD FALLS ASLEEP IN HER BED. AND IF IT'S TRUE THAT PEACE IS FLEETING, THAT IN THE FUTURE THEY WILL AGAIN BE THREATENED BY DRAGONS, AND WITH THEM ALL MANKIND, IT IS ALSO TRUE THAT IT'S A BEAUTIFUL NIGHT. A GORGEOUS NIGHT!
THE END

COVER
GALLERY

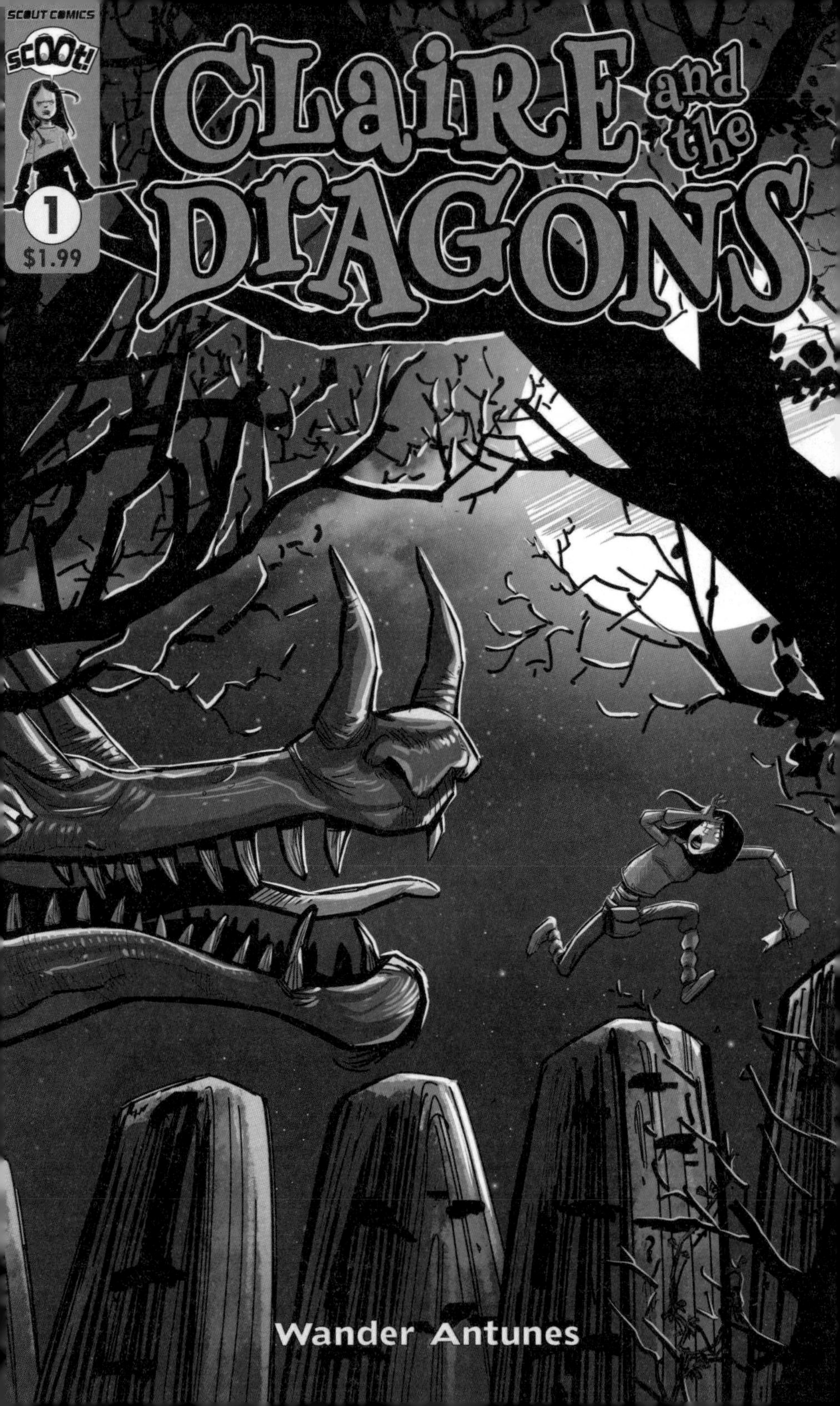

SCOUT COMICS
SCOOT!
1
$1.99
CLAIRE and the DRAGONS
Wander Antunes

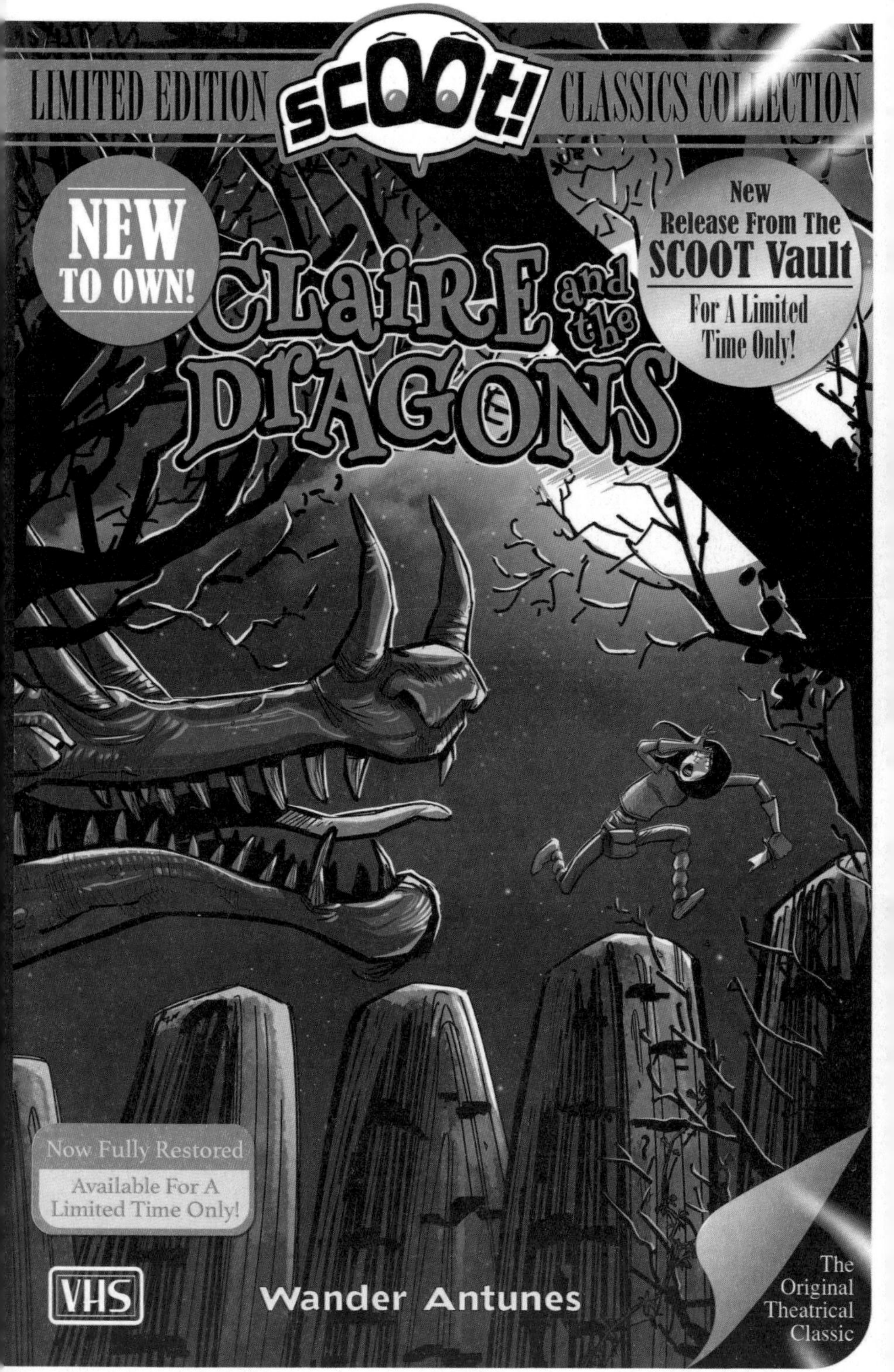
LIMITED EDITION
SCOOT!
CLASSICS COLLECTION
NEW TO OWN!
CLAIRE and the DRAGONS
New Release From The SCOOT Vault
For A Limited Time Only!
Now Fully Restored
Available For A Limited Time Only!
VHS
Wander Antunes
The Original Theatrical Classic

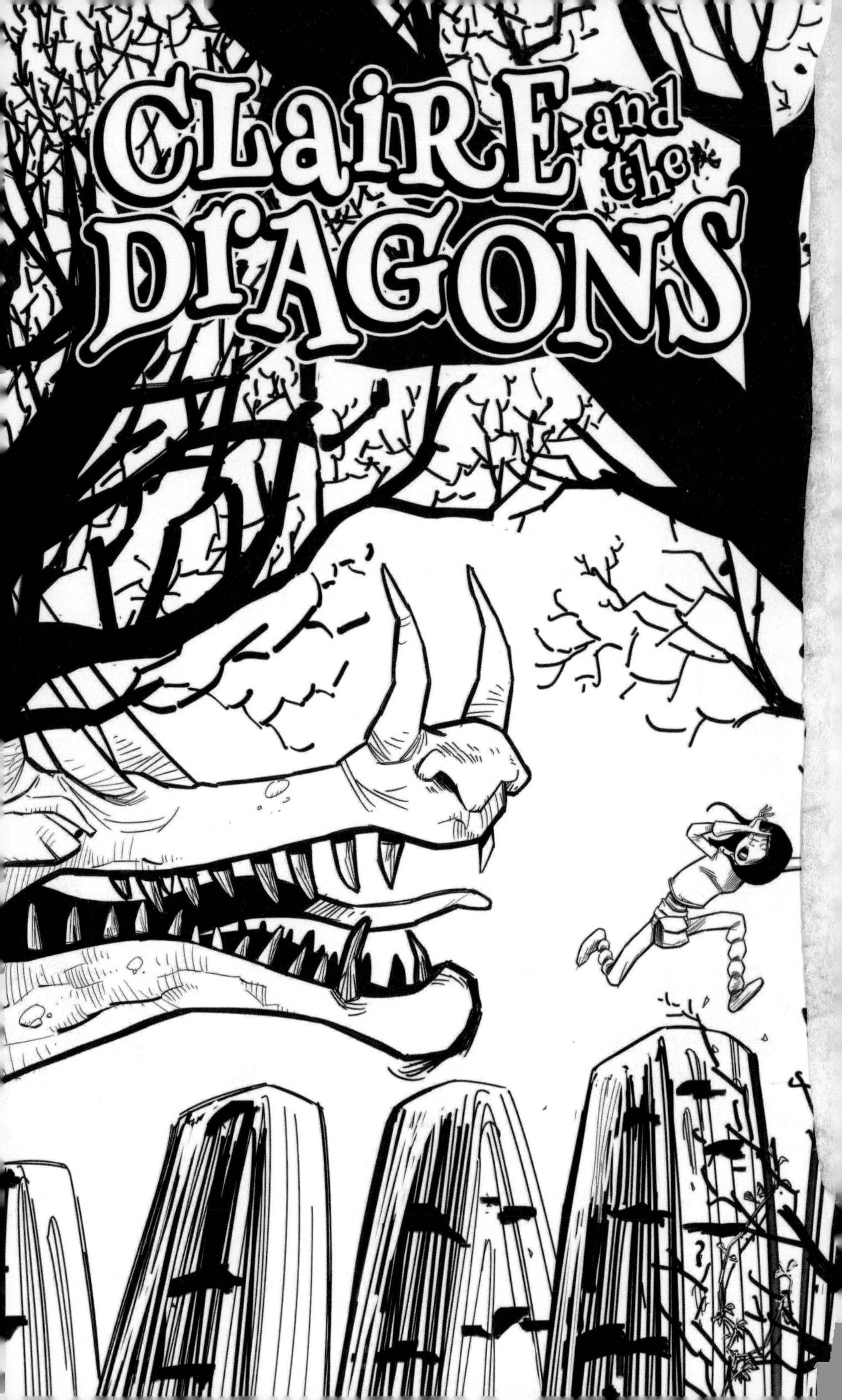
CLAIRE and the DRAGONS

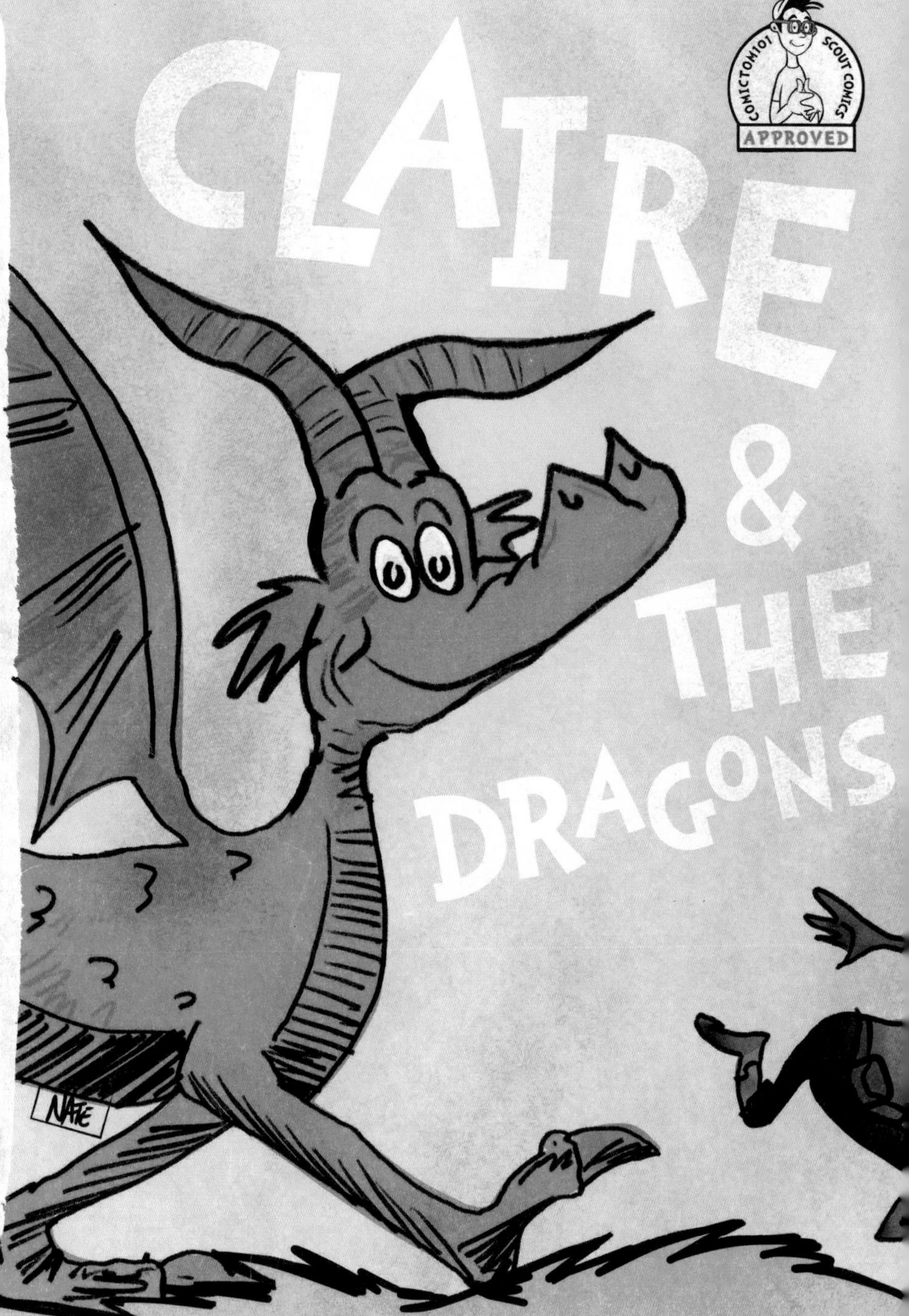
CLAIRE
&
THE
DRAGONS
COMICTOM101 SCOUT COMICS
APPROVED
NATE

A comic book project

By: WANDER ANTUNES

CLAIRE & THE DRAGONS

A comic book project by
WANDER ANTUNES